Murder By Appointment

Murder By Appointment

An Inspector Faro Mystery

Alanna Knight

G.K. Hall & Co. • Chivers Press
Thorndike, Maine USA   Bath, England

This Large Print edition is published by G.K. Hall & Co., USA
and by Chivers Press, England

Published in 1997 in the U.S. by arrangement with
Curtis Brown UK.

Published in 1997 in the U.K. by arrangement with
Macmillan.

U.S. Softcover   0-7838-8044-8   (Paperback Collection Edition)
U.K. Hardcover   0-7451-8903-2   (Chivers Large Print)
U.K. Softcover   0-7451-8904-0   (Camden Large Print)

The text of this Large Print edition is unabridged.
Other aspects of the book may vary from the original edition.

Set in 16 pt. Plantin by Rick Gundberg.

Printed in the United States on permanent paper.

British Library Cataloguing in Publication Data available

Library of Congress Cataloging in Publication Data

Knight, Alanna.
    Murder by appointment : an Inspector Faro Myster / Alanna
  Knight.
    p.   cm.
  ISBN 0-7838-8044-8 (lg. print : sc)
  1. Large type books.   I. Title.
  [PR6061.N45M87   1997]
  823′.914—dc21   96-45511

For
Patrick Tilley

Chapter One

Detective Inspector Faro extracted himself with difficulty from the crowd of Edinburgh concert-goers leaving the Assembly Rooms that evening.

His air of preoccupation had less to do with the splendid rendering of the Beethoven Sonatas he had just heard, than with the identity of their performer Lachlan Brown, the talented young Highlander who had sprung to fame and international acclaim during the last three years.

Still deep in thought Faro negotiated Princes Street with its thin line of carriages, some carrying prosperous families homeward, some with curtained windows discreetly drawn against the curious. The occupants he guessed would be heading towards Leith Row's notorious howffs where their night's entertainment and revelry was about to begin. Other carriages were driven at reckless pace by arrogant young students with too much wealth and too few manners, as they hurled abuse at those pedestrians who tried in vain to cross the busy thoroughfare.

Stepping aside in the nick of time, Faro regarded his narrow escape in disgust. He would have liked to snatch down some of those grinning youngsters and give them a good shaking. However, dignity prevailed. Decorum must be maintained by senior policemen.

Vaguely declining the offer of a lift from one of his stepson's medical colleagues, he headed up the Mound and away from the main traffic, walked rapidly homeward in the direction of Newington.

At last his pace slowed and, taking stock of his surroundings, he sighed deeply. Late spring with its burgeoning of new life in every garden and hedgerow was his favourite season.

The evening was perfect with the promise of longer sunny days in store and, as he climbed the hill, moonlight outlined the castle far above him touching its windows with uneasy life, as if Queen Mary and those sad apparitions of her short and tragic reign still stalked its corridors.

But it was the spectre of a time nearer to his own that haunted Faro. For once his thoughts had nothing to do with crimes, ancient or modern. Guilt perhaps, but definitely not crime as the Edinburgh City Police understood it.

As he walked his footsteps echoed the final chords and the rapturous applause of Lachlan Brown's recital, the two encores before the audience would release him.

Faro had observed it all closely from the most expensive seats. A vantage point from which not only the piano and the pianist's hands were clearly visible but, what concerned him more, the young man's face. The young Highlander had outstanding good looks, black hair, olive skin, full mouth and wide dark eyes. And listening to the brilliant performance Faro continually scanned that coun-

8

tenance, minutely searching for some resemblance to a well-known face, other than the one he had last glimpsed in Ballater several years earlier.

He remembered the rumours concerning Lachlan Brown. In addition to undeniable talent, his spectacular rise to fame was the hint that he was 'an intimate relative of John Brown, the Queen's favourite ghillie and protector'. The bolder ones took it further, with hints that Brown was Her Majesty's unofficial husband whose public acknowledgement would sweep her from the throne and that Lachlan was Brown's illegitimate son from a youthful indiscretion the Queen was prepared to overlook.

Faro knew that to be untrue. He had it from the lips of the boy's mother. Lachlan's paternity might be in doubt but John Brown was definitely not his father.

He had almost reached the top of the Mound when, with the suddenness that characterized Edinburgh weather, the moon was obliterated by fast-moving clouds.

'Stepfather!' The brougham stopped by him and Dr Vince Laurie leaned out. 'Jump in!'

Olivia, Vince's wife, looked pleased as she made room for him. 'We usually go via the Pleasance, but we've just set down brother Owen in Heriot Row. He's staying with friends —'

'I do really enjoy the walk, my dear,' Faro protested weakly.

How to explain that the evening solitude of quiet streets was his favourite time of the day and

9

walking was his own special way of solving problems, criminal or personal, or that a wealth of experience had produced nothing better for clearing the head than a brisk Edinburgh wind.

'Are you sure?' said Olivia anxiously, regarding the sky. 'It's going to rain.'

In two years of marriage, the young woman, who never took a step in town if it could be avoided or a carriage was at hand, continued to be baffled by her stepfather-in-law's eccentricities.

'And why a policeman who walks considerable distances each day in pursuit of criminals can possibly claim to enjoy walking for pleasure is quite beyond me,' she told Vince on frequent occasions.

Vince, however, understood a great deal about his stepfather that his wife had yet to learn.

Now he turned to her and laughed. 'Give up, Livvy, do. You'll never persuade him.'

Faro glanced at the sky above and shook his head. 'Not unless the heavens open, and I don't really think that is very likely.'

'Be it on your own head, Stepfather,' said Vince, knowing he would never be able to convince dear Livvy about Faro's preference for going to concerts alone when she, fearing that he might be lonely, anxiously begged him to join their group of friends. Useless to try to explain without giving offence that he wished to enjoy and appreciate the music with single-minded devotion. And without the polite distractions offered by the frequent passage of boxes of chocolate and opera-glasses. Olivia on the other hand regarded such interruptions as a necessary part of an amiable social occasion.

Saluting the departing carriage, Faro followed in its wake. Quickening his pace, absorbed by his thoughts, he was hardly aware that gentle moonlight had been replaced by swift-moving storm clouds.

'Damnation!' he exclaimed as the first heavy raindrops splashed down and, diving for shelter into the nearest doorway, he watched helplessly as the cloudburst filled the gutters to overflowing, a channel of water soon flowing past him.

At last the sound he most wanted to hear. An approaching vehicle! From the direction of the Mound, the familiar shape of an Edinburgh hiring carriage had him leaping out of his sheltering doorway.

Signalling it to stop and thankfully about to climb aboard, he heard the sound of footsteps behind him.

A breathless voice sobbed out, 'Help me, sir. I implore you, please help me.'

Turning, he saw a middle-aged woman, shabbily clad. Her cloak and bonnet were dripping wet and she carried neither umbrella nor reticule. As she spoke, she held out trembling hands to him.

Cursing his ill luck at being faced with the predicament of someone with a need obviously greater than his own, he gallantly stepped aside and with

11

a bow murmured, 'By all means, madam —'

But instead of accepting his offer and stepping into the carriage, she shook her head violently and clutched at his arm.

'Please, sir — I beg you. I'm in terrible danger —' And, pausing to glance over her shoulder, 'Please, try to understand. Those men — they're going to kill me —'

Faro followed her pointing finger, squinting against the driving rain. He could see no one, but the poor woman was clearly overwrought. He decided to humour her.

'Of course, of course.'

'Thank you, sir, oh, thank you. God bless you, sir.' The accent was familiar and brought a fleeting sense of recognition.

As he leaned forward to help her into the carriage, two shadows emerged from the darkness. Two large heavy male shadows, breathing deeply as if they had run a considerable distance in search of their quarry.

Faro's position, with one hand assisting the woman up the step into the carriage and his back towards the two men, put him at a considerable disadvantage. The arm he thrust out was an instinctive movement, completely ineffectual to fend off the stout stick raised high in the air above him.

It descended in vicious contact with his skull.

As he heard the agonizing crack that splintered the night into sickening blackness, his last thoughts were: 'Now I'll never know the truth about Lachlan Brown.'

Chapter Two

A nauseous headache told him that he was still alive.

He could take dubious comfort from that but was considerably surprised to find himself in his own bedroom in 9 Sheridan Place. His first thought was that the incident on the Mound had been one of the violent nightmares to which he was prone, paying dearly for something carelessly eaten that disagreed with his faulty digestion.

The pain as he moved and touched the bandage about his head told him otherwise.

A movement at the window indicated Vince hovering near by.

'So you're awake. Thank God for that. I thought you might be heavily concussed.'

When Faro groaned, Vince continued cheerfully, 'I should know something of the thickness of your skull by now. It's saved you many a time when lesser mortals would have met with certain death. I suppose it's that old Viking stock you have to thank —'

'What happened?' Faro demanded weakly.

Vince smiled wanly. 'Well, I was rather hoping you could give me the answer to that.'

'I was attacked. I fell for the oldest trick in the book, lad. A woman in distress pleading with me while her confederates crept up from behind.'

Vince looked at him quickly. 'Not like you to be fooled by that one, Stepfather.'

'I thought I'd seen her somewhere before. That was what foxed me.'

Vince was aware of his stepfather's remarkable memory for faces. 'And had you?'

'Aye, back in the mists of time, the devil knows where.'

But that was not the only reason, he thought. If my mind hadn't been wrestling with Lachlan Brown's identity, my wits would have been sharper. And none of this would have happened.

As they were speaking the hall clock struck midnight.

'Just an hour ago,' said Faro. 'Seems more like a hundred years. How did I get here? Who brought me home?'

Vince put a hand on his shoulder. 'We did. The rain was so torrential, I decided we should go back for you. You couldn't have travelled very far and were probably taking shelter.'

He shrugged. 'You may laugh, Stepfather, but I had one of my weird flashes — that you were in some kind of danger, and from more than pneumonia. I thought I was being an idiot —'

He grinned apologetically but Faro knew better than to doubt Vince's strange intuitions which had saved them both from disaster in the past.

'Lad, thank God you did come back.'

'Livvy thought I was mad when I told Briggs: Back to the Mound. The rain had ceased, quick as it came. When there was no sign of you Livvy insisted you'd got a carriage and we'd missed you. But no carriage had passed us and none had we met. There was no sign of you. Then we saw what looked like a bundle of clothes in a doorway. It moved — I saw a hand — you know the rest,' he added grimly.

There was silence for a moment then Faro asked, 'All right, what did they get? I suppose they took everything of value.'

Vince handed him the jacket which hung over a chair. Faro went through the pockets. But none of his possessions was missing. His gold watch and chain, his leather notebook were there, also a purse of six sovereigns, very worthwhile pickings for any attacker. As was the gold wedding ring belonging to Vince's mother, which Faro carried next to his heart. It had been with him since the day he took it from her dead hand as she lay in her coffin beside their stillborn son.

'Nothing taken. All intact,' he said.

Vince looked puzzled. 'Are you sure?'

'Absolutely sure.'

'If it wasn't robbery, then what was their motive?'

The two men were silent for a moment, then Vince said, 'When you're up to it give me precise details and I'll report your injury to the Central Office. Presumably they'll want to track down these villains.' He paused. 'If they didn't take anything, could this be revenge perhaps? Your last case as I remember was a bit tricky.'

'All now safely behind bars, I assure you.

Give me a pipe, will you.'

As Faro struggled to sit up, Vince protested, 'I'm not sure that you should, Stepfather — I don't think —'

'You're not required to think in this instance. But I damned well am. So give me a pipe, when you're told,' he added sharply.

A few moments later Vince said, 'If only you'd been able to see their faces.'

'At least I won't forget the woman's again, once I remember where we last met,' said Faro grimly. 'I'll certainly recognize her next time, that's for sure.'

'But what was the motive, if it wasn't robbery or revenge?' Vince persisted. 'You must bear in mind that it might not necessarily be recent. After all, you must have made a lot of enemies over the years. It might be some villain recently released. Could it be that you had this woman's husband — or lover — put away? Could you have seen her in court?'

Faro thought for a moment and shook his head, a gesture that pained him exceedingly. The effort of dredging up memory involved a mind that seemed unable to function.

'What are we left with, then? Hardly desperation for a carriage,' said Vince with a wry attempt at humour. 'I know they are hard to come by in Edinburgh at the best of times and especially in the rain —'

Faro puffed steadily at his pipe before laying it aside. 'There are several possibilities and one in

16

particular that I don't care to contemplate.'

'You mean that the woman who appealed to you for help might not have been a trap?'

'Precisely. She might have been in genuine danger. If so, God only knows what her fate was.'

'What about the carriage — and the coachman?' Vince asked.

'He was either bribed or in league with them. Perhaps I wasn't the fare he was told to uplift but, blinded by the rain and so forth, he made a mistake.'

Attempting to swing his legs out of the bed, Faro stood up shakily. 'I'll see if there's anything been reported at the Central Office.'

'Hadn't you better wait until morning, Stepfather? You're in no condition to travel anywhere —'

'I'm in no condition to listen to medical advice, either, so let's get moving —'

Faro walked unsteadily across the room, clutched the bedpost for support and said weakly, 'Get me a carriage, will you, lad. Now don't argue, do as you're told. And I won't disturb Briggs at this hour.'

'Look, Stepfather, just stop being stubborn. It's for your own good. A day or two of rest and you'll be fine. You're not forgetting that Rose will be arriving at teatime. You don't want to distress her, by her seeing you like this. Now, do you?' he appealed.

Rose.

Faro had momentarily forgotten Rose. The adored elder daughter whose intent upon what he considered an unsuitable marriage was his main domestic problem. The night's events had thrust her from his mind. And for once Faro allowed himself to be led back to bed, the covers firmly tucked about him.

'Here, drink this,' said Vince.

'A dram, is it?' he said hopefully.

'It is not. A mild sedative that will ensure you sleep soundly.'

Faro drank and leaned back against the pillows.

Rose. She mustn't see him like this. He must be fit, his wits sharp to deal with her arguments. He closed his eyes. Visions of Lachlan Brown mingled with rain, and melodies from the Beethoven Sonatas.

Aye, the newspapers had got it wrong about Lachlan.

And, as he was drifting into sleep, he heard a woman crying for help. He was back on the Mound again, a woman's white face staring up at him, terrified. He tried to sit upright, stretch out a hand to help her. But Vince's sedative had turned his arms to water.

That face. His pride and boast was that he never forgot a face. And the woman — the woman. Had he seen her before?

A scene jogged across his vision. He almost had it, but even as he tried to put it into sharper relief, it vanished.

Yes, he had seen her before. Somewhere in the untidy depths of memory, she was there.

But where — when and where?

Chapter Three

Against Vince's professional advice, Faro presented himself at the Central Office of the Edinburgh City Police the following morning. His
appearance, two hours later than usual, aroused
some whispered speculation among the young
constables on duty outside.

Faro, fully aware of their interested attention,
made a firm progress up the steps, his hat pulled
well down over his forehead to conceal Vince's
bandage. Considering the soreness of his head
and the unsteadiness of his legs, he was grateful
for his stepson's insistence that Briggs drive him
there in the brougham.

'Anything to report?' he asked the man on desk
duty.

The constable looked at his list. 'Three break-
ins, two cases of assault, three of soliciting, oh
aye, and at five this morning, a woman's body —
carriage accident apparently.' He looked up.
'Bastard hadn't even stopped —'

'Where is she now?'

'Down below, sir. Don't you want the rest?' he
added with another look at the list of minor
crimes.

But Faro was already heading swiftly along the
corridor down the stairs that led into the chilly
depths of the police mortuary. A grim place

where, at the discretion of the police surgeon, unclaimed bodies became the property of his medical students after three days for the purpose of dissection.

After all Faro's years as a policeman, the fate of unidentified sheeted corpses lying there never failed to chill his soul.

Today there was only one body on a trestle in solitary isolation in the middle of the room.

Dr Nichols, the police surgeon, looked up from his desk and greeted the Inspector cheerfully. His rotund body, white hair, luxuriant beard and rosy cheeks plus the permanent frown between his eyebrows suggested a genial Santa Claus who had found himself in the wrong role.

He removed the sheet as requested and Faro found himself looking down on the face, now tranquil in death, of the woman who had pleaded in vain for his help and protection.

'They are going to kill me —'

The sombre words echoed in his head. Ashamed that he had believed this unfortunate woman had set him up for a gang of thieves, he touched the sleeve of his coat as if to ward off the memory of those frantic clawing hands. If only he had reacted with more speed. If only his normal awareness of danger had not failed him.

He sighed; his life story seemed characterized by those fatal words: If only . . .

'Brought in early this morning,' said Dr Nichols.

'So I was told. What about her injuries?'

The doctor shrugged. 'Consistent with being run over by a carriage. What one would expect. Here — and here —' He drew the sheet down further. But Faro hardly listened.

'Was there any possibility that she was already dead?' he asked, cutting short the doctor's clinical details. 'I mean, before the accident?'

The doctor knew Inspector Faro and his reputation too well to regard this question with surprise.

'Wheels run over her were enough to kill her. Did plenty of damage — liver spleen, ribs — see for yourself —'

Faro averted his eyes from the mangled corpse. 'Do we know who she is?' The doctor shook his head and Faro sighed. 'Any clues to her identity?'

'You can see what we have for yourself.' As Nichols signalled to his assistant, Faro remembering the woman had been empty-handed, knew the answer. And if she had been murdered, as he suspected, her killers, in their own interest, would have made certain she carried no means of identification.

As they waited, Nichols looked at Faro. 'Murder, sir. Is that what you have in mind?' And he spilled the bag of clothes out on to a spare trestle. 'This is what she was wearing.'

Faro unfolded a black cloak and a grey merino dress. Even in better days undrenched by rain, they would have been shabby and threadbare. They were, however, neatly patched. The linen undergarments, chemise, petticoat, drawers, repaired and carefully mended, the stocking feet well darned. The condition of her clothes and the stitching indicated that their late owner was of a careful disposition, either a seamstress of some ability or lady's maid. The excellent quality of once-fine linen indicated that in all probability they had been passed down to her by some grateful well-off employer or benefactor. Her hands, neither rough nor red, were further confirmation of his suspicions.

'That's all there was, Inspector. No reticule. Perhaps it rolled away somewhere. We'll never know. Nothing here to tell us who she might be, sir.'

But the doctor too had come to his own conclusions. 'All the signs indicate a member of what we like to call the respectable poor, sir. Servant, like enough, I'd say.'

Faro agreed but with some cautious reservations, based on bitter personal experience. Clothes did not always tell the truth and could be deliberately misleading. As he had found to his cost in the Case of the Missing Duchess.

'Let me see.'

He studied the woman's face carefully before Nichols replaced the sheet. The doctor looked puzzled at the intensity of Faro's gaze.

'Something I missed, Inspector?'

Faro shook his head. 'No. I thought when I first saw her that we had met before.'

'And have you?' said the doctor hopefully.

When Faro shook his head, the doctor smiled.

23

'You must have a good memory for faces, sir.'

'Goes with the job, doctor. But I'm afraid it has let me down this time. No matter. Tell me, were there any marks besides those of the wheels?'

'Then you are suggesting this might be murder, sir?'

Without going into the details of the assault on himself, Faro nodded. 'Could be.'

The doctor whistled. 'Rum business, Inspector. That mighty crack on the back of her head might not have been contact with the carriage wheel, or the ground when she fell.'

Faro winced, remembering the heavily nobbled stick, the kind carried by desperate men who meant business, rather than a gentleman's accessory, as the doctor continued, 'Her skull was fractured.'

'Would that be enough to kill her?'

'Yes, of course. But I must point out to you that this injury is also consistent with the carriage accident.'

'Where was she found?'

'In Dean Village.'

Faro looked up. 'Hardly a busy thoroughfare. Not exactly the hub of the heavy carriage trade at five in the morning.'

The doctor sighed. 'The assumption is always that the driver was one of those young blades, reckless — and drunk.'

Pausing, he regarded Faro earnestly. 'You know it as well as I do, Inspector. These young well-off lads will do anything to avoid trouble, bringing discredit on their families and so forth. Manslaughter is a difficult tag to have to live down if your heart — or your family's heart — is set upon seeing you as advocate — or doctor — or minister of religion.'

But Faro was hardly listening. Dean Village was on the other side of the town, far beyond the Mound and the Georgian New Town with its staid streets and crescents of elegant houses.

Thanking the doctor for his help, he returned grimly to his own office upstairs. The time that had elapsed and the distances involved suggested that after the two men's murderous assault on him, the woman had been similarly treated and was already dead or dying before the carriage accident was staged.

He shuddered and touched the bump on his head tenderly. If his skull hadn't been thick, then he might have been occupying the adjacent trestle in the mortuary.

'Bound to happen to him with his kind of life. All the enemies he made. All the villains he put away. Just got unlucky, that's all. You can't win for ever —'

Such would have been the verdict of his colleagues. With a funeral service in St Giles, laid to rest in the quiet grave beside his beloved Lizzie, he would have been luckier in his demise than the dead woman. The fate of unknown corpses at the hands of medical students, although necessary for the progress of medical science, continued to trouble him.

There was nothing he could do to avert the inevitable. Unless he could produce evidence before the Procurator Fiscal within three days that the woman had been murdered and produce an identity, and a family who would make the necessary funeral arrangements, he would be left with another unsolved murder on his hands.

Vince had insisted that Briggs bring him home again and Faro was not displeased to be carried back to Sheridan Place where the smells of baking greeted him as he opened the front door. Rich fruit cake and roasting meat assured him that Mrs Brook was preparing a banquet fit for his daughter Rose. With the assistance, sought or unsought, of the new maid, May.

Faro sighed. Rose's imminent arrival presented problems momentarily more pressing than the dead woman's identity.

As for Mrs Brook's behaviour, he suspected this might indicate a smouldering volcano threatening his peaceful domestic scene. Once in sole command of her two gentlemen, she had warmly welcomed the young mistress but, apart from dark glances, kept her own counsel, refusing to be drawn on Mrs Dr Vince's contribution of a mute servant into the household, despite the girl's tragic history.

Chapter Four

As Faro eagerly anticipated Rose's arrival, he realized her future was a major preoccupation. Rose and his determination to keep her away from Detective Sergeant Danny McQuinn, who as a young constable, had been for some years his right-hand man. Together they had solved many cases, put many criminals behind bars and, on more than one occasion, he had owed his life to McQuinn's speedy intervention.

Faro tried not to remember such indebtedness since Danny McQuinn had become the love of Rose's life. The two were like magnets, each forever drawing the other. According to Rose, she had loved Danny (so she claimed) since she was twelve years old and he rescued her from an abduction attempt on one of her visits from Orkney where she and her younger sister Emily had lived with his mother since Lizzie died.

Faro had been tolerant of what he considered childish hero worship for the handsome young Irish policeman, an infatuation he was certain that Rose would outgrow. But she had proved him wrong and despite all his attempts to matchmake on her infrequent visits to Edinburgh, by introducing her to agreeable, eligible and highly desirable young men such as Olivia's brother, Dr Owen Gilchrist, he realized that she had no romantic inclinations towards any other man than Danny McQuinn.

It was aggravating and Faro acknowledged that he was helpless to change the course of his daughter's lovelife until a hitherto unseen opportunity offered itself for an assistant detective in the ranks of the Glasgow City Police. A splendid chance for promotion and he immediately recommended McQuinn for the post.

McQuinn was touchingly grateful for this boost to his career and Faro had the uncomfortable satisfaction of knowing that his not entirely altruistic action had succeeded in parting the two lovers.

Relief was short-lived when Rose wrote to him that she had obtained a teaching post in a Glasgow girls' school. He did not doubt that McQuinn was the reason for her leaving Orkney and, worst of all, that he no longer had ways of keeping them from seeing each other, or indeed of playing chaperon.

Vince was not sympathetic. His two-year-old marriage to Olivia had made him more aware of romantic possibilities for less fortunate couples. He refused to understand why Rose should not be allowed to make her own choice and follow her heart's desire, especially when that desire was reciprocated.

'Don't try to play God in people's lives, Stepfather,' he warned Faro. 'Especially those close to you. You'll get no thanks.'

And Faro wondered if Vince ever realized now how desperately his stepfather had willed the match between himself and Olivia, or of his sly attempts at matchmaking. Vince would never know how Faro had despaired at his 'long friendship' with Olivia and her twin brother Owen when she was so obviously the perfect wife.

He had almost given up hope when, to his amazement, Vince casually announced that he and Olivia were to marry. And it was Olivia who refused to listen to Faro's suggestion that he move into a smaller apartment in one of the tenements near the Central Office where many of the unmarried constables lived.

His protestations that a young couple should begin married life on their own were scornfully swept aside.

'Not another word from you on that subject, if you please,' Olivia said firmly. 'This is your house and we are greatly obliged to you for allowing us to share it.'

And with a smile, a warm kiss on his cheek, she added shyly, 'Besides, we would miss you dreadfully. And Mrs Brook. Whatever would we do without her? We'd never find a housekeeper like her again. It will take May years and years — she's so inexperienced. We're relying on Mrs Brook to train her.'

Mrs Brook remained silent on the subject of May, the maid whom Olivia's aunt in Stirling had rescued from the workhouse. The aunt's recent death had left the girl destitute, orphaned as a small child, robbed of parents and siblings in a house fire, her powers of speech destroyed by the terrifying experience.

Kind-hearted Olivia provided the perfect solution without having ever met the lass who had been well trained as lady's maid but whose efficiency below stairs was somewhat limited. She also failed to realize that Mrs Brook jealously guarded her realm and was exceedingly possessive regarding her supreme reign over 9 Sheridan Place.

Faro treated such trivial domestic episodes as matters of no importance. They were strictly for a housekeeper to sort out while, above stairs, he basked in the harmony of Vince and Olivia's happiness. Daily he marvelled that his stepson's present bliss bore no resemblance to the previous condition of the young man forever losing his head to some unsuitable woman.

Joy and pride in his pretty, clever wife had transformed Vince into a solid, respectable Edinburgh doctor, with a thriving practice of respectable middle-class patients.

Even the frivolity of his fair boyish curls now thinning rapidly gave his slightly balding appearance an extra dimension of solid reliability.

If Faro was grateful for anything, it was that his younger daughter Emily showed every indication of making an early but entirely suitable marriage to a wealthy Orcadian widower of ancient lineage whose family had owned and farmed the land for more than two hundred years. A romantic tale of nursemaid to motherless child about to become lady of the manor.

If only Rose had shown such initiative. His joyful anticipation of her visit was tinged with secret anxiety. Although Danny McQuinn's name was never mentioned, by common consent and their mutual affection for each other, where nothing was allowed to disturb the harmony of their rare meetings, he did not fool himself regarding that silence. Sooner or later he must face the inevitable: on one of these visits, he would hear the words he most dreaded.

The scene was so engraved upon his mind that he often awoke in the middle of the night, scarcely able to believe that it had not already taken place. Seeing Rose's laughter suddenly fade, as she whispered, 'I have something to tell you, Papa. Danny and I are to be married.'

For his part, Faro had rehearsed and discarded many attempts at how he would react. How he would put a brave face on it, wishing them well and hiding his bitter disappointment. He could do no less, for Rose was eighteen and no longer needed his consent.

'Disappointment?' Vince had queried. 'I should have thought that Danny's future prospects as an inspector were admirable.'

Faro shrugged impatiently. Vince had always liked Danny and was now prepared to take his side in this domestic matter.

'I don't want Rose to be a policeman's wife. I hardly thought you needed reminding of the hazards involved,' Faro protested weakly.

'Surely she is best qualified to decide what kind of a life she wants, Stepfather. Or what kind of a husband.'

Faro winced at the word. Vince saw through his subterfuges and he was guiltily aware that his stepson guessed he wanted Rose to make a 'good' marriage and that Danny McQuinn, a bog Irishman and a devout Catholic who went to Mass regularly, was not quite the ticket for a chief inspector's daughter.

Faro had never questioned her on the delicate matter of their differing religious beliefs, for if his daughter's wavering doctrine wasn't strong enough, he had himself to blame. He had hardly set a good example through the years since his appearances in church were dictated only by the decorum of deaths, marriages and ceremonial police occasions.

Rose and Emily had fared no better in Orkney with his mother who had severed any connection with the established church after the murder of Faro's policeman father. She had reverted to the almost pagan beliefs in the God of the early Celtic Church which had predated both Catholic and Protestant. Neither one had done anything good, according to Mary Faro, but set men at one another's throats. With such unconventional upbringing Rose could hardly be expected to let religion interfere with marriage to a man she loved.

He was writing up his log on the unknown woman when the doorbell clanged cheerfully through the house.

Rose was here.

He looked at his watch. He hadn't expected

her until teatime and thought delightedly that she had caught an earlier train.

Finishing the sentence he was writing, he heard Mrs Brook's footsteps on the stairs. Wondering, he rose from his desk and crossed the room as the housekeeper tapped on the door and announced, 'A gentleman to see you, sir.'

And Faro found himself face to face with almost the last person he ever expected to see in his house.

The newcomer was Lachlan Brown.

'I do apologize for disturbing you, sir.'

'Not at all. Please take a seat.' And watching him narrowly across the table, Faro was conscious of his own confusion and anxiety at this totally unexpected visit.

The years since they last met had turned the handsome but sullen youth into an uncommonly good-looking man. He had an undoubted charisma, especially with the distance between concert platform and auditorium removed.

'May I take this opportunity of congratulating you on your performance of the Beethoven Sonatas?'

Lachlan looked pleased. 'Why, thank you, sir. So you have been to the Assembly Rooms.'

'I have indeed. And it is a great pleasure to meet you.'

'Not for the first time, Mr Faro. But I don't suppose you remember?'

'Oh yes. At Glen Gairn.'

Lachlan frowned. 'Not a happy occasion. I hope you have not had many such Royal hazards to cope with.'

Faro dismissed the suggestion with a gesture, aware that plots to kill the Queen such as that he had been investigating were fairly commonplace for the police, especially with an unpopular monarch. Such information, however, was not for the likes of this young man.

'Uncle John — Mr John Brown, that is,' said Lachlan consolingly, 'He takes jolly good care of Her Majesty.'

'So I believe,' said Faro drily and Lachlan's glance was not altogether innocent as he continued hastily, 'That must be a great relief for everyone.'

He guessed that Lachlan could not be unaware of the scandalous rumours that drifted down from Balmoral. Tales of an indiscreet association between the Queen and John Brown, and of late-night drams in the Royal bedroom with her favourite ghillie performing the services of a lady's maid and putting her to bed.

It was not the first time that widowed Scottish queens had been enamoured of commoners but it fitted ill into the stern moral code Victoria wished to impose on the mass of British society.

'Mr Brown is well?' said Faro to break the uncomfortable silence.

Lachlan brightened. 'Oh yes, very. I visited him at the beginning of my tour. When I was in Aberdeen.'

Again he fell silent, inspecting one of his fingernails as if it was in imminent danger of disintegration.

Faro continued to watch him, his polite smile becoming fixed as he wrestled with the burning question: What on earth was Lachlan Brown doing here in his study just two hours before his next appearance at the Assembly Rooms?

And as if he had heard the unspoken question, the young man's head jerked upright. Leaning forward he said, 'I suppose you are wondering what brings me to your door instead of directly to the police station, Mr Faro. I'll come to the point. It's like this, sir. Someone is trying to kill me . . .'

Chapter Five

'Someone is trying to kill me . . .'

The words reverberated in Faro's mind, touching echoes of the woman who had recently died.

Lachlan Brown watching his expression laughed uneasily. 'You see, someone took a pot shot at me last night as I was leaving the Assembly Rooms.'

'Were you hurt?'

'No, no. Not at all. He — whoever it was — missed me by inches. I think a rifle was used and fired from a passing carriage.' He paused and sighed. 'My guardian angel must have been hovering. You see, it was windy when I closed the door and I dropped one of my sheets of music — a new piece, one I'm composing. I had stayed on to rehearse it since the piano in my lodging is pretty deplorable. Anyway, as I bent to pick it up, I heard the shot —'

Again he stopped, shuddered as if remembering, and diving into his pocket he threw a bullet down on the table. 'There!'

Faro picked it up. 'Remarkable. But tell me, how did you come by this?'

'If it had hit the stonework, and ricocheted I'd never have found it. But I noticed the woodwork of the door jamb behind me was splintered and I dug it out.'

'With great presence of mind, may I say,' said Faro, picking up the bullet and rolling it between his fingers.

Lachlan beamed on him. 'Yes, wasn't it?'

Faro decided that the young man was either very brave or exceedingly foolish as he asked, 'Were you not afraid whoever shot at you might return when they saw they had missed their target?'

Lachlan shook his head. 'I suppose they thought that they'd got me. I went straight on to the ground — and stayed there — when I heard the shot.'

'Very quick thinking on your part. And highly commendable in such circumstances.'

The young man smiled wryly. 'I've travelled in some lawless towns in America during the last year. I know something about guns — and gunmen.'

'Well, well. Do you indeed?' Faro considered the bullet in the palm of his hand. 'And have you any idea then why anyone should want to kill you?'

Again Lachlan shook his head. 'I have my off moments like most musicians.' His laugh was without merriment as he continued, 'However, I have never considered that I gave a bad enough performance to merit being murdered for a poor rendering of the Beethoven Sonatas.'

'So there are no enemies that you can think of?'

'None that I know of, aforesaid passionate music lovers excepted.'

37

'No jealous rivals who might pay someone to get rid of you?'

Lachlan laughed. 'Good Lord, no, Mr Faro. I'm just an average good musician — I'm not a genius. There are many as good, even better than I am. But to be frank with you, they don't have the publicity of a somewhat notorious Royal association.'

'Come now, you are underestimating your talents. I have heard you play —'

Lachlan made a dismissive gesture. 'As far as I'm concerned it's a big world, Mr Faro. There are a lot of concert halls to fill, room for an awful lot of good pianists.'

Faro smiled. He liked this young man. He had a refreshing honesty and no airs and graces. A tribute to John Brown's down-to-earth no-nonsense influence.

'I presume there must be some reason why you did not immediately summon the police. And you should have done so as it might have been possible to track them down —'

'You know the answer well enough, Mr Faro. Imagine how it would have sounded in the newspapers. The billboards would have had a heyday: "Protégé of John Brown in mystery murder attack." And that is putting it very mild indeed. My imagination can stretch much further,' he added shrewdly, 'As I am sure, sir, can yours.'

Faro was silent as Lachlan continued, 'We have all heard the rumours concerning a Royal person. And that is the kind of publicity I do not care to court. I can fill my concert halls adequately without that kind of notoriety, thank you.'

But Faro's mind was racing ahead. He was thinking of that other murder carriage in the Mound. And the dead woman who had begged for his assistance. Was this another, less successful attempt by the same assassins? And if so what was the connection between a poor serving woman and Lachlan Brown?

'Tell me, did anything strange — I mean out of the ordinary routine — happen that night before you left the theatre?'

Lachlan thought for a moment. 'Nothing important. As you can imagine, I am exhausted, pretty shattered by the end of a performance. I give it all I've got, my entire being, all my concentration as well as tremendous physical effort. I had also been working on a new piece — my own composition. I was very excited about it as I'd just thought of the last few bars, how exactly it should end, that very morning walking in Princes Street Gardens. With the recital over, I was longing to work on it. That was why I stayed on.'

'Did anyone know of your plan?'

'No. It was quite spontaneous. Spur-of-the-moment decision.'

How then had the assassins known? Had they been lying in wait for his eventual emergence from the Assembly Rooms? That would not have been difficult as there were always carriages waiting for fares in George Street late at night.

'I frequently get supper invitations,' Lachlan continued, 'but I prefer to go back first to my hotel, for a wash and a change of linen.' He frowned and then exclaimed, 'Now I remember! There was something different last night.' At Faro's hopeful expression he sighed, 'Not very helpful and not in the least sinister, I assure you.'

'No matter,' said Faro. 'Please go on.' There was always the possibility of a lead, no matter how improbable the circumstances.

'Well, I was about to leave when an oldish man popped his head round the dressing-room door. A fan, it seemed, who had got past the attendants.'

He smiled. 'But this one was from long ago. He introduced himself, but I didn't get his name. Davy — Mac-something or other. But it seemed he was a great friend of Uncle John's. They had grown up together in Glen Gairn and he had known me when I was a wee lad. Did I not remember him? he asked. He had carved a wee boat for me to sail in the burn. I remembered the boat clearly but not the giver, alas. You know how it is with young children,' he added apologetically.

'I felt particularly ungrateful because he was obviously on hard times. He said he was living in Edinburgh now and when he saw my name on the board outside, he felt impelled to look in for auld lang syne. As he was talking I saw how shabby he was, a thin worn jacket two sizes too small for him, obviously a hand-down, a thread-

40

bare muffler round his neck. Frankly, he looked like a frail old beggarman you'd meet any day on the High Street.'

He shrugged. 'He showed no signs of leaving and in one of those rather long and embarrassing silences when neither of us could think what to say next, I asked politely if he was a music lover — presuming, of course, that he had been at the performance. The poor old chap blushed, studied the floor intently and mumbled that a shilling was more than he could afford and even if he understood music, the fiddle was as far as it went with him. As for a shilling, well, that would buy him food for a week.

'I knew I had guessed right, and the real reason for his visit was obvious. He was hoping I might give him some money. That was what he was leading around to, but too proud to do more than hint. I was damned sorry for poor old Davy. I had a jacket hanging on the back of the door, one of these horse-blanket things, violent red and yellow checks, I was given in America by a fan. I only brought it with me because I know from bitter experience that hotel bedrooms and empty concert halls, when I'm rehearsing, can be very chilly.

'I saw him eyeing it. It was thick and warm and I knew I'd never have a better reason for disposing of it or to a better cause. So I gave it to him. He put it on there and then, hugging it to him. The violent colour didn't seem to bother him. I thrust a sovereign into his hand to go with it. He protested weakly but I could see he was delighted — and grateful. As he was leaving, he turned and said, "God be good to you, Mr Lachlan. And you be careful, take care, take good care." When I laughed and said indeed I would, he was suddenly very serious. He took my hand and said, "I mean it, young sir, you watch your step. Be very, very careful." '

Lachlan sighed. 'In view of what happened a few minutes later, his words might well have been prophetic, don't you think?'

An interesting encounter, or a coincidence? Was Lachlan putting too much meaning into the man's parting words?

Apart from the carriage there was little evidence to connect Lachlan's attackers with those on the Mound. As Faro was thinking of a suitable reply, the hall clock melodiously struck the half-hour. Lachlan shot out of his seat.

'I really must go, Mr Faro. I've taken up enough of your time and I'm late for my rehearsal.' He paused. 'Thank you for listening to me. I shall leave it all to your discretion — I mean, what if anything I should do about it.'

He smiled. 'I thought it was only in the American West that men drove along those streets and took pot shots at passers-by. I've told myself that perhaps it was some drunken revellers here — young blades, I think they call them.'

Faro regarded him sternly. Drunken revellers there were, but armed drunken revellers were something new and unique in Edinburgh. 'You can dismiss that theory from your mind. I don't think these bad habits have crossed the Atlantic into Edinburgh — particularly into George Street. There's plenty of room in our cells for those sort of lads,' he added grimly.

'So you think I should report it,' said Lachlan reluctantly.

'I will look into the matter personally. And I will do my best to see that it is not made public.'

'I'll be grateful, Mr Faro.'

As Faro rose from his desk, he felt there was still a great deal unsaid, unsayable, and that the would-be assassin's identity masked a sinister purpose greater than jealousy or revenge. But what?

Preparing to part, the two shook hands. Lachlan hesitated then said quietly, 'I had another reason for coming to you, sir. My mother — my mother said that if ever I found myself in danger or in trouble of any kind, you were a friend I could rely on and that I was to come to you.' Again he paused. 'My mother thinks highly of you, Mr Faro. Very highly.'

A now thoroughly confused Faro was spared the embarrassment of thinking of a suitable reply as, about to ask politely after Inga St Ola's health, he was interrupted by the front doorbell pealing shrilly through the house.

'I must go,' said Lachlan. 'Goodbye, sir, and thank you again.'

There was a sound of light footsteps, familiar footsteps, on the stairs. The door was thrown

43

open and Rose Faro flung herself into her father's arms.

'Dear Papa. How are you —' And thrusting aside her bonnet to release a cascade of fair curls, she was suddenly aware that they were not alone.

Lachlan Brown moved out of the shadows.

'You! —' Rose stared at him and a moment later laughed delightedly as he rushed forward and seized her hands.

'This is wonderful — I can't believe it —' said Lachlan.

As the two young people stared at each other with astonishment and delight, Faro announced, 'This is my daughter Rose.'

Chapter Six

The young couple hardly heeded Faro's introduction.

Still holding Rose's hand, Lachlan looked across at Faro: 'Yes, of course, now I do see a resemblance.'

'You have met before?' Faro's polite question was by now somewhat superfluous.

'We have indeed,' said Lachlan warmly. 'So this young lady is your daughter — Rose. Rose,' he repeated, smiling as if the name pleased him. Turning again to Faro, he said, 'Forgive me, I really must leave. I'm already late —' And to Rose, 'May I see you again? Now that I've found you?' he added gently.

She smiled. 'Of course. I'll be here with Papa until the end of the week.'

Lachlan bowed over her hand. 'Dinner is out for me, I'm afraid. But lunch at the Café Royale, perhaps?'

'That would be lovely.'

Lachlan smiled ruefully. 'Where I was brought up, dinner was the midday meal, but here in Edinburgh it's *de rigueur* to call it luncheon.'

Rose laughed. 'It's the same in Orkney. Breakfast, dinner and supper. No one's heard of luncheons yet!'

They had forgotten Faro whose mind wrestled

45

with a fast-moving kaleidoscope of thoughts, none of which gave him any cause for complacency. It was obvious that the two were very attracted. At one time he would have welcomed Rose's distraction from Danny McQuinn, especially for a concert pianist and composer, a cultured young man with a great future.

But with one of fate's little ironies, Rose had been presented with the one man she might never marry.

'A very pleasant young man,' he said as the front door closed and he wondered what bitter destiny had brought them together.

Rose was eager to tell him. 'He is so nice. I'm glad you think so too, Papa.' So his suspicions were correct.

'I've heard him play. He's very talented, you know. Did you meet at one of his concerts?'

Rose smiled. 'Goodness, no. We met on the Aberdeen train for Glasgow. I'd spent Easter at Orkney, as you know, with Gran and Emmy. The boat was late disembarking and I had only about ten minutes to get from dock to railway station. Naturally there wasn't a carriage in sight. I took to my heels and the guard had blown his whistle when I raced on to the platform. Someone — Lachlan — threw open the door, stretched out a hand — but just then the strap on my luggage broke. You know what I'm like when it comes to packing. Well, everything spilled out on to the platform. I was so embarrassed. Books, papers — clothes — everywhere.

'But Lachlan took charge of the situation, leaped out, commanded the guard to hold the train, gathered up all my belongings and bundled me into his carriage. I was very grateful. He was so charming and we talked all the way to Glasgow.'

She paused for breath, her eyes shining, remembering.

'Without any exchange of names, I take it?' said Faro.

'There seemed no need as we were fellow travellers, together for an hour and unlikely ever to meet again. Talk of Aberdeen led to Deeside and that he had been brought up there. I said I went there for holidays long ago. You know how it is, Papa,' she added dreamily, 'how you can meet a complete stranger and within minutes be telling him the story of your life.

'It wasn't until the train pulled into the station at Glasgow and I saw people rushing forward to greet him on the platform, I guessed he was someone of importance. So I quietly disappeared. And then I read in the newspapers about his background, the scandal about being Brown's illegitimate son, and I realized that I had been travelling with Lachlan Brown, the famous concert pianist.'

She made a face. 'He mentioned vaguely that he played the piano and to my everlasting shame I remembered saying how interesting, so do I! Wasn't that awful! Anyway, I never expected to see him again — and now this, finding him in my father's study. I can hardly believe it. Is he a friend of yours?' she added eagerly.

'Hardly, although I greatly admire his playing. He was just bringing me greetings from old friends at Crathie,' Faro lied cheerfully. Rose would hardly appreciate that her rescuer was being used as target practice for some maniac with a rifle.

'I am so pleased,' said Rose. 'Makes it a lot easier, doesn't it, for us to meet when he is, well, almost a friend of the family. And talking of family, where are Vince and Olivia?'

'Vince is visiting sick patients and Olivia busy with one of her charities, I expect. She is involved in so many good works, I've lost count.'

Rose laughed. 'She is wise to enjoy them while she may, I'm afraid babies will change all that.' Pausing, she glanced round the study. 'Nothing ever really changes in Sheridan Place. It's good to know that home stays the same. Is Mrs Brook reconciled to sharing her domain with Olivia's maid? I haven't met her so far . . .'

Faro put his finger to his lips. 'You'd better ask her yourself,' he whispered as footsteps outside the door announced Mrs Brook's arrival and for the next few moments he witnessed a great deal of hugging and laughter between the normally reserved housekeeper and the girl to whom she was completely devoted.

At last pausing to draw breath, Mrs Brook smoothed down her pinafore and her hair and gave Faro an embarrassed smile. 'I didn't hear the front door close, sir, and I wondered how many there would be for tea.'

'Just ourselves, dear Mrs Brook,' said Rose.

'Very well.'

Rose held the door open for her and with a backward glance at her father said, 'I'll come with you.'

Faro's guess that this was curiosity to meet the maid was confirmed when Rose arrived with the tea tray.

'Have you taken over Mrs Brook's duties?'

Rose laughed. 'I insisted, Papa.'

'This is the brink of a new era indeed.'

She shook her head. 'That poor lass. To be so afflicted. I felt heartily sorry for her. And I get the feeling that Mrs Brook doesn't like her much.'

'Indeed? What did she say to you?'

Rose smiled ruefully. 'Mrs Brook doesn't need to say a word. She can convey a whole dictionary of disapproval in one small sniff and toss of her head! I don't think it's personal, she just dislikes this intrusion in her domain. As I was leaving the kitchen, the girl staggered in with a load of shopping. Such a tragic face. You can tell she's had a hard life and suffered a lot. As if she's still having difficulties keeping all her nightmares at bay.'

'Nightmares?' Faro queried.

Rose shrugged. 'Her terrible childhood experiences are written all over her face. I was amazed at how young she is. Not much older than me, but she looks nearer thirty than twenty. Don't you think so?'

Faro had to confess that he hadn't noticed. He

observed little of what took place in the kitchen regions of his house. As long as his meals were on hand when he wanted them, his laundry cared for and his bed made — and most important, his study left untouched by duster or polish — he was well satisfied. When he met the girl she was either very shy or afraid of him; like a forest creature she was poised for instant flight. Now he took evasive action, merely nodding and wishing her good day.

'Olivia's told me about the fire that killed all the poor girl's family,' said Rose. 'She must have been in that orphanage a long time before she went to Aunt Gilchrist.'

'I don't know any of the details,' Faro said and Rose's glance made him ashamed. A champion of the underprivileged, human or animal, she had been so obviously moved by the plight of the dumb servant and, without saying a word, conveyed to her father that he should make it his business to find out and take a great deal more interest in those less fortunate members of society who sheltered beneath his roof.

He patted her hand. 'I'm sure she's well cared for. Olivia is responsible for her and she's a very caring person.'

Rose sighed. 'You're right, of course, you are. She smiled and returned again to the exciting news of her sister Emily's forthcoming marriage.

Watching Rose as she tackled Mrs Brook's afternoon tea with its sandwiches, Dundee cake and scones, Faro decided she was a sight to refresh and delight any eyes: the fair curls clustered modishly around her forehead, the deep blue eyes with long dark eyelashes, short nose, full mouth and healthy complexion — although he was not quite so sure about the fashionably elegant curves of a corseted figure for one so young.

Nor could he credit the resemblance that Lachlan had observed. Rose was truly Vince's sister and grew more like her mother every day. She had inherited his own Viking colouring and he liked to think some of his better qualities, but what delighted him most was her look of his dear Lizzie who would never be dead as long as Rose lived.

As for Lachlan Brown. He was definitely Inga St Ola's son.

Rose's first day at home passed happily, re-united with Vince and the sister-in-law with whom she had much in common. Faro was de-lighted that he was able to spend the evening with his family as they talked and played cards and Rose's sweet voice accompanied Olivia's playing of the pianoforte she had brought from her old home.

When at last the lamps were put out and the house was in darkness, he drew his curtains against the night. Moonlight touched the garden and beyond it a ring of bright stars crowned the lofty heights of Arthur's Seat, leaning like a lion couchant against the horizon.

Faro sighed as he settled down to sleep and

thought with envy of men like himself all over Edinburgh whose destiny lay in uneventful lives in banks and offices and who came home each night to suppertime where a rare evening such as he had enjoyed was a commonplace event.

Breakfast was a meal Faro had seldom shared with Vince before his marriage. Neither man was at his best at seven in the morning, both finding it difficult to be sociable. Of necessity Vince's habits had changed with marriage and now, by tacit agreement, he and Olivia breakfasted in the dining room waited upon by Mrs Brook, whose first duty was to bring a tray to Faro's study.

As Faro was having his second cup of tea, Rose looked round the door. 'May I disturb you, Papa? No, I've eaten already, thank you,' she added as she kissed him. 'See what the postman brought me!'

Lachlan Brown had been good to his word and the envelope she thrust before Faro contained a ticket for his concert with a short note inviting her to a supper party with some friends afterwards.

Rose's face glowed with pleasure and excitement. Misreading her father's anxious expression, she said, 'Perhaps you would like to come with me. I'm sure Lachlan wouldn't mind. Or would you be bored?'

'Bored with music? Never, lass. And if Lachlan had wished me to accompany you, then he would have sent another ticket. However, I'll take you to the theatre.'

He had a very good reason for so doing. He wished to inspect the lintel of the Assembly Rooms door which Lachlan claimed had been splintered by the rifle bullet.

As he escorted Rose up the front steps the mark, which had passed presumably unnoticed by the caretaker, was clearly visible more than a foot above his head. Whoever had fired the bullet had severely misjudged his target, considering that Lachlan, like Faro, stood a little over six foot in height.

That fact gave Faro some thought as to the significance of the apparent attack.

Misjudged. Or merely a warning?

Chapter Seven

Faro set off for the Central Office next morning, faced with an unpleasant duty: a further visit to the mortuary, where he hoped that his growing suspicions would prove incorrect and that the dead woman had been removed by grieving relatives or friends.

She had not.

And she was not alone. The trestle alongside was occupied by the corpse of an elderly man, the sheet being replaced by Dr Nichols who had just completed his examination.

'Brought in this morning, Faro. Constable Thomas has all the details.' The doctor looked up briefly. 'Another case for you, I'm afraid.'

'Indeed?'

'Died within the last twenty-four hours. An attempt has been made to suggest that he had died in his bed, perhaps of natural causes such as cardiac arrest.'

'What do you mean — "an attempt has been made"?'

In reply Nichols removed the sheet and invited Faro to inspect the man's skull. 'See for yourself. He was hit very hard on the back of the head. The second fractured skull we've had in this week,' he added grimly nodding towards the woman's body. 'Seems catching.'

And but for the grace of God, as Faro knew his mother would say, it might well have been three. Himself included.

'Any identification?' Faro asked Thomas who had appeared at the door where he was disposed to linger. His wary glance towards the two bodies indicated that he shared his superior officer's distaste for mortuary visits.

Keeping his distance, he took out a notebook. 'Found in a lodging house in Weighman's Close, sir.'

Faro knew the area off Leith Walk, poor and squalid, a shilling a week would provide a roof over a man's head and little more.

'He's a Mr Glen, according to the landlady. That's all she knew about him, or was willing to tell her. Except that he wasn't from these parts — from up north somewhere, she believed.'

As Thomas spoke, the doctor's assistant produced a brown-paper bag and shook out a pathetic bundle of worn and none-too-clean clothes, patched and darned.

'This is what he was wearing, sir. Looks like an old beggarman.'

Faro was studying the man's face intently.

'A moment, Doctor, if you please.'

Removing the sheet from the dead woman's face, he remembered that her accent had been familiar and Lachlan Brown's talk of Glen Gairn had jogged a further chord of memory.

Turning to Dr Nichols, he asked, 'Look at these two. Tell me, do you see a remarkable resemblance between them?'

The doctor glanced over Faro's shoulder. 'In what way?'

'Could they possibly be related?'

Dr Nichols shook his head. 'All corpses look alike to me, I'm afraid.' His slightly exasperated tone suggested that Detective Inspector Faro was being more eccentric than usual and that his hopes of a nice tidy disposal of the two corpses in the direction of his medical students was doomed to failure.

Faro motioned to the constable, who came forward reluctantly. After a careful scrutiny, eager to oblige, he said, 'You might be right, sir. They do look a bit alike. Same sort of bone structure. The woman looks younger, though there's probably not much in it. Another murder on our hands, sir?'

As they approached Weighman's Close by way of the quayside, the crews of two ships moored alongside were the target of good-natured catcalls from the fishermen unloading their catches to a screaming accompaniment of seabirds.

The *Royal Solent*, a handsome yacht, bound for the Isle of Wight, was frequently used by members of the Queen's entourage or visitors to Balmoral who could afford the luxury of a more congenial means of reaching Osborne House than the tortuous rail journey to the south coast of England, followed by a short but often unpleasant crossing of the Solent.

The second ship was the *Erin Star*, sailing between Edinburgh and Rosslare, for wealthy passengers of a similar disposition to those on the *Royal Solent*, who, anxious to avoid a journey by train and the notorious Irish Sea crossing, wished to enjoy a voyage — good weather permitting — to Southern Ireland in relative comfort.

Faro remembered that one of Constable Thomas's recent tasks had been to arrest a stowaway who was carrying with him the proceeds of an Edinburgh jewel robbery. It had been one of the constable's first cases undertaken alone.

'You did very well on that one,' said Faro, nodding towards the ship. 'From what I read in the report, you showed considerable initiative — and courage. Well done, Constable.'

'Thank you, sir.' Thomas beamed. 'But I did have a bit of luck too and good timing, coming by the information unexpectedly,' he added modestly.

Earnest and ambitious, Thomas was new enough to the job to welcome exchanging the dull and mostly sordid daily routine for the possible excitement of a murder hunt, as Faro discovered when he enthusiastically led the way into the lodging house.

'I found the dead man upstairs in a back room face downwards on the floor, sir, and he didn't look to me like a man who had died of a bad heart. I know, sir. I've had some experience of heart attacks. I was with my grandfather when he died,' he added triumphantly as they ran upstairs.

57

On the landing he turned to Faro and said, 'And the motive couldn't have been robbery.'

'What makes you so sure of that?'

Thomas laughed. 'You'll soon see for yourself. Nothing worth the stealing. Wait till you see the hole he lived in,' he added, opening the door of a bleak impersonal room furnished with the transient characteristics of most cheap lodgings in the city. A rickety-looking bed with patched thin cover held pride of place beside a broken wooden chair, and a tin cup and saucer on a derelict washstand.

Faro felt disgusted that anyone paid money for what was little more than a prison cell, especially when he opened the wall press. The empty shelves were covered with dirt and stains accumulated over the years by many former tenants plus a strong suggestion that its present ones were of the rodent variety.

At his side Thomas sniffed the air. 'God, sir, even the mice must have a lean time existing here.'

The sorry condition of the man who had drawn his last breath in the squalid room was confirmed by a complete absence of possessions of any kind.

'Looks like he was in a hurry, sir. No intentions of staying any longer than whatever his dubious business dictated,' said Thomas.

Faro nodded. This was the kind of room he associated with criminals on the run. He regarded the constable with approval. Here was a young policeman who caught on fast. He would go far, he decided, watching him examine the window, which rattled in the ill-fitting frame while a piercing draught issued from the direction of the Firth of Forth.

'That's how whoever topped him got in, sir.'

About three feet below the sill, a washhouse roof and a drainpipe would have presented little difficulty of access to a determined murderer.

'It could have had benefits both ways,' he told Thomas. 'For a criminal on the run, as well as a killer. Look —' he pointed to the broken lock. The sash window opened with a minimum of effort. 'We had better speak to the landlady.'

But she was already hot on their heels, panting up the stairs, demanding to know who they were and what they were doing wandering about a respectable house without permission.

As Thomas stepped forward from behind Faro, she was somewhat mollified by the familiar sight of the policeman's uniform, for this was the same constable who had arrived on the scene when she rushed out screaming for help, yelling that there was a dead man in her house.

When the man in plain clothes was introduced as Chief Inspector Faro, her aggressive manner vanished and, anxious to placate them and make a good impression, she suggested they adjourn downstairs to her own premises.

Faro was surprised after the sordid scene he had left upstairs to find himself in a well-furnished spacious parlour where nothing had been spared for personal comfort in the way of cushions, highly padded sofas and a good burning fire.

A locked glass cabinet carried the usual insignia of the Edinburgh middle class, china ornaments, crystal and silver.

Mrs Carling was also well furnished with jewellery and as well upholstered as her velvet sofas, her frizzled hair a shade of red that nature had never invented. She obviously did well out of her poor lodgers, thought Faro, as she invited the policemen to a glass of wine, which they refused. The gesture made, she sat down opposite and addressed them in sepulchral tones.

'That this should happen in my house. It is quite unbelievable — poor Mr Carling must be turning in his grave —'

As Faro listened he had a feeling that such tragedies among the poor who rented her rooms upstairs were perhaps not all that infrequent and that poor Mr Carling's eternal rest might often be so disturbed.

She was at pains to emphasize that she ran a respectable boarding house for impoverished gentlemen and Faro could no longer restrain his impatience with the self-righteous monologue as she stressed her virtuous tolerance and warm humanity. She was not pleased to be cut short by Faro's sharp questions concerning the deceased.

'Mr Glen came to us three weeks ago. He lived very quietly —'

'I understand he was not from these parts —'

'That is correct. From somewhere up north, he was.'

'Then what was he doing here? Did he have a job?'

Mrs Carling bristled at that. 'He did not have an occupation that I was aware of.' She sat straight. 'I don't enquire about my gentlemen's business. That is their own affair. As long as they pay their rent regular and behave with decorum —'

'Criminals often pay their rent and behave with decorum.'

'I'm very particular about my gentlemen.' Her voice was heavy with outrage. 'Mr Glen was a very reserved, quiet boarder. Otherwise I would have sent him packing. There now.'

She paused to eye the constable sternly and her gaze drifted towards Faro, conveying the unmistakable impression that the pair of them might well not have met her high standards.

'I trust my gentlemen implicitly. They have their own keys and the staircase is used by all of them.'

'So you wouldn't be aware if Mr Glen had any visitors last night?'

'Visitors are strongly discouraged, Inspector,' Mrs Carling said stiffly. 'This is a respectable house,' she repeated.

Discouragement was hardly needed, for why anyone should find comfort or welcome in visiting such a room as the late Mr Glen had occupied was something Faro would have enjoyed debating at some length.

'Did anyone call on him during his tenancy with you?'

The woman's face shadowed. 'There was one woman — earlier this week. She looked about the same age as himself, on the elderly side. But she was tidy, neat, respectable-looking, well spoken. I wouldn't have let the other kind across my threshold,' she added sternly.

'Be good enough to define respectable-looking?'

Mrs Carling shrugged. 'She looked like she had fallen on bad times, they both did, come to that. I'd have put her down as a maid in upper-class service, or a shop assistant. You meet a lot of her kind in Princes Street every day of the week —'

Before she could go off at a further tangent, Faro asked, 'And how long did this visitor stay?'

'A while. She was very agitated, upset. I was cleaning the staircase,' she added, shamelessly aware that she had been overcome with curiosity about the woman. 'I heard their voices raised. Arguing, perhaps. Money, most likely.'

'Money? What made you think it was money?'

'I heard her saying something like it was too little and that they should get more for it. Whatever it was, he told her to keep her voice down and that he wouldn't give it to her. Said it was too valuable.'

Faro looked at the woman with grudging admiration for her tenacious eavesdropping.

'It certainly wasn't a lovers' tiff that's for sure,' she continued. 'They just weren't the type for such goings on.'

'Indeed?'

Mrs Carling laughed. 'Oh, yes, indeed. I've had plenty of elopers and absconding husbands and wives meeting illicit lovers in my time. I can spot them right away, I can assure you.'

'So you think there was a disagreement about money?'

'Oh yes, indeed. You see, I asked for my rent a month in advance. Cheap at the price, it is. There is a splendid view of the Castle from that particular room. One of the best in the house.'

Faro shuddered. God help the others then, he thought as she continued.

'Mr Glen hinted that he didn't have a situation at present. Kept himself very much to himself, as I've said,' she added regretfully. 'However I got the distinct impression that, like the woman who visited him, he might have been an upper servant at one time.'

'Indeed? How did you reach that conclusion?'

'Well, I've been in high service myself, before I married Mr Carling, that was. I don't mind admitting it. But I always kept myself respectable,' she added proudly. 'That's how I got where I am today —'

'You were telling us about Mr Glen,' Faro reminded her.

'He asked a lot of questions about servants' conditions, what wages they got and so forth, over there — in the New Town,' she added, pointing in the direction of Georgian Edinburgh.

'And when did you last see Mr Glen?'

'Since he was behind with his rent and due to

pay another month in advance, he was very keen to avoid me on his way in and out. But I heard him come in on Tuesday night and I was ready and waiting for him. He said he had no money. When I asked what he intended doing about it, he had the nerve to offer me a jacket in lieu of payment —'

'A jacket?'

'Aye, a new jacket. Never worn, he said. I didn't like the idea, a man's jacket. Well, he might have stolen it. Especially when I saw it —'

Faro thought rapidly. 'May I see this jacket, if you please?'

'If you want.' She left them to return holding the garment before her. 'See for yourself,' she said proudly. 'As I said, I wasn't keen at first but it's good quality, clean and warm. And I realized it would be just the thing for my lad when he's a bit older —'

The jacket was bright red with yellow checks.

Faro held out his hand and, almost reluctantly, she handed it over, watched him suspiciously as he inspected the lining. As if to confirm his suspicions, a label read: 'Chicago Textile Mills. United States of America.'

She watched him turn out all the pockets.

'You'll find nothing there,' she said defensively. 'I've already had a good look in case there might be a paper with an address of relatives.'

Faro looked at her. 'No coins or anything like that?'

She coloured slightly but shook her head.

She was lying, for the jacket he held answered the description of that given by Lachlan Brown to his visitor from Glen Gairn, and Faro had a sudden vision of the two dead faces lying side by side in the mortuary.

The possibility that they were related brought alarming implications that somehow the woman's death and the attack on Lachlan Brown were related and that the beggarman's visit and his parting warning was no coincidence. Merely the curtain raiser to a deadly game.

Chapter Eight

Before Faro could question the woman further about the jacket, the door opened and a well-grown youth of about thirteen came in.

Despite his mother's attempts at gentility, her careful accent as she explained quickly that the gentlemen were enquiring about poor Mr Glen, Andy Carling had the wily look and attitude Faro was well used to encountering, that of the Edinburgh street urchin, born and bred.

'Andy often went messages for Mr Glen,' said Mrs Carling, obviously glad of this diversion.

'Aye, that's right. He wasna' too keen on using his own feet and legs. Didna' go out much during the day.'

'What kind of messages?' asked Faro.

'Food and once a letter.'

'Who was this letter addressed to?'

'A Miss McNair.'

That was interesting, thought Faro, as Mrs Carling interposed, 'I said to Andy that was probably the woman who visited him.'

'Can you remember the address by any chance?'

Andy exchanged a glance with his mother.

'These gentlemen are policemen and this is Detective Inspector Faro,' she said. 'They want us to help them.'

This revelation was followed by a look of guilt and anguish towards his parent, a glance that plainly asked: Was there money involved? Shall I oblige or not? Then deciding there was no doubt profit to be gained, he smirked at Faro and with a self-important air that marked him as Mrs Carling's son, he said, 'I canna' mind the exact address, but I can take ye there, sir. It's nae far: Duddingston way.'

Faro recognized that he had had an unexpected stroke of luck, although there was only one person who could identify the jacket as once the property of Lachlan Brown and confirm 'Mr Glen' as his mystery visitor Davy, friend — or so he claimed — of John Brown.

Faro folded the jacket and put it beneath his arm, cutting short Mrs Carling's protests. 'This is required to help establish the dead gentleman's identity. It will be returned to you.' And, tearing a page out of his notebook, he wrote rapidly. 'Here is a receipt.'

Andy regarded this procedure with dismay, especially when Faro, laying a hand on his arm, suggested that he accompany them to Duddingston.

Clearly afraid that he was being placed under arrest, Andy began to tremble, and yelled, 'Ma!'

Muttering reassuringly, Faro did not relinquish his grip on the lad's arm. Andy was bundled inside the police carriage beside Constable Thomas, his nervousness increased at being thus anchored between guardians of the law.

'What was this lady like?' Faro asked, as the carriage trundled through the streets.

'Oh, just an old lady, ye ken.'

'How old would you say?' asked Faro patiently.

'Older than you. Grey hair. No' frae Edinburgh, either.' And gazing steadily out of the window, he pointed. 'Over there. That's it.'

The tiny cottage of recent vintage was deserted, its windows blackened ominously.

There had been a fire and the smell of smoke hung unpleasantly upon the air.

As they stepped down from the carriage, Andy was not disposed to linger. With one panic-stricken glance at the scene he took to his heels and raced along the road back towards the city.

And what was strangest of all about his precipitous departure was his neglect to wait for any reward for his services.

The fire had been recent enough for their presence to attract an immediate investigation by next-door neighbours and two small elderly ladies of almost identical appearance hurried towards them. Obviously sisters, white-haired, with spectacles over noses twitching with curiosity, hands fluttering in dismay and eyes wide and eager. Their emergence struck Faro with a striking resemblance to a couple of squirrels from the nearby woodland.

'It happened two nights ago —' said the first.

'No one was hurt, Mary,' said sister number two. 'That's right, sir. The lady who lived there —'

'Who lives there, Annie,' sister Mary corrected her.

'A Miss McNair —'

'They'll need to trace her, to give her the news.'

'What a shock for the poor soul.'

A shock for the searchers too, thought Faro, when they discovered she was dead, and in all probability murdered.

'How did the fire start?' he asked.

Two heads shook in unison.

'Miss McNair was a very careful lady.'

'Oh, she was, indeed. Not the kind Annie and I would associate with neglecting fires.'

'But sparks do come out, Mary. These chimneys are bad on downdraughts. Remember we had our fireside rug burnt.'

'And if we hadn't been in the room, goodness knows. Our cottage might have gone up in smoke many a time.'

'That's why we are always particularly careful with the fireguard, isn't it Mary —'

'We are from the police, madam. And this is Detective Inspector Faro,' said Constable Thomas, interrupting what showed signs of becoming an interminable flood of reminiscences.

'We are looking for Miss McNair in connection with one of her relatives recently deceased,' said Faro.

Relief flooded the two upturned faces. Police obviously suggested criminal activities in this gentle neighbourhood.

If only he and Thomas could investigate without attracting undue speculation, but the two sisters watched them relentlessly as Faro tried the front door.

It was locked. As he was wondering how to broach the subject of a spare key, sister Mary approached and said, 'The back door is open. The lock was broken when Miss McNair moved in and she's never had it repaired.'

'Besides no one here ever locks their back doors, Mary.' And turning to Faro, Annie continued, 'She's only been here a short while and keeps herself to herself. Doesn't she?' she added to her sister.

As did Mr Glen, thought Faro grimly, with no longer any doubts that Lachlan Brown's 'Davy Mac-something' would also prove to be a McNair.

Picking their way through the two rooms, they saw that although the interior of the kitchen had been seriously damaged, its contents had survived the conflagration as a depressing array of blistered furniture and scorched rags of curtains.

'Look over here, sir,' said Thomas.

The fireplace showed evidence of papers having been burnt in the grate. Faro regarded it thoughtfully. One spark would have been sufficient to ignite the worn rug and spread fire through the house.

That the two dead people were brother and sister was confirmed by Miss McNair's few possessions. In the bedroom press, darned underwear indicated an original owner with expensive tastes in body linen.

He examined the stitches. Sewing styles were

highly individual and he had a feeling that the same hand had also mended the beggarman's darned clothes.

The lack of any documents or letters suggested that further evidence had been carefully destroyed, but returning to the kitchen he found Constable Thomas still meticulously raking through the ashes in the fireplace.

'Looks as if an intruder might have been searching for something. When he couldn't find it he deliberately started the fire to cover his tracks, sir.'

The two sisters were at the door, awaiting the policemen's emergence from the cottage.

'Did Miss McNair have many visitors?' Faro asked.

Mary shook her head. 'We only saw two callers, didn't we, Annie, all the time she was here.'

'That's right. And both came when she was out.'

'And what were these visitors like?' asked Faro, expecting either a description of Mr Glen or of the two men who had abducted Miss McNair and undoubtedly murdered her.

'They came at different times —'

'Yes, that's right. One was a young man, the other a young woman.'

'Young, you say?'

'Yes indeed. And they were from Ireland.'

'Ireland — are you sure?' he asked.

'Well, they spoke with Irish accents,' said Annie.

71

'We know because our mother came from Kerry,' said Mary triumphantly.

So much for his theory, thought Faro as he asked, 'What did this young man look like?'

The sisters regarded this question as odd. They studied Faro carefully as they replied, 'Oh, well-spoken. Twenty-five or so —'

'About your height, sir. Spectacles and red hair —'

'And the young woman?' asked Faro.

'She was tall and slim, good-looking too, wasn't she, Annie?'

'Well, yes. That is, what we could glimpse of her face through her veil.'

'We thought she might be a charity worker or a nurse.'

'Definitely not a servant, that's for sure.'

'A real lady.' Annie repeated. 'Educated, well-spoken — like the young man.'

Faro decided the conversation was getting nowhere, so much of it built on speculation. He was disappointed too since the two callers would most likely prove to have nothing to do with the McNairs' deaths.

Summoning Constable Thomas, he headed towards the police carriage. The two sisters followed, anxious to prolong this drama which had invaded their usually uneventful lives.

'There was one other person, Inspector,' said Mary.

'Who was that?' demanded her sister sharply.

'You've forgotten, Annie. There was the other

young woman wanting to know if the cottage was for sale. She was looking in the windows,' she explained to Faro. 'We saw her and, well, we were curious.'

Annie gave a sigh of exasperation. 'It was a mistake,' she said to Faro. 'It was the cottage further down the road she was interested in. She was just wanting directions, nothing to do with Miss McNair, Mary,' she added crossly.

'I know that, but she did ask who lived there,' said Mary. 'And when we told her it was Miss McNair, a single lady and as far as we knew she hadn't any plans to move, she said even if it had been available it was too small for her with a husband and four bairns. I just thought the Inspector should know, Annie. He did ask about all visitors.'

'But the last woman wasn't a proper visitor, she was just a passer-by,' her sister protested.

'Well, you were the one who thought it was odd having three Irish people all practically on each other's heels —'

Thankfully Faro and Thomas left them still arguing. As the carriage headed back along the lochside, the constable said, 'That Carling lad took off very sharpish, sir. I was just thinking, did he know something? Or was it a natural fear of being associated with arson?'

'You could be well right,' said Faro grimly, pleased that Thomas also had sharp powers of observation and had recognized a villain in the making.

Thomas gazed out of the window. 'There's something else, sir. If those two in the mortuary are related — and I agree with you, there was a strong resemblance. Assuming they were brother and sister, why were they not sharing the cottage? There were two rooms after all, if you count the box-bed in the kitchen.'

Faro gave Thomas an admiring glance, for the same idea had occurred to him.

'Perhaps they had something to conceal, some criminal activity that linked them.'

'That's right, sir. And by living together they each put the other in danger.'

Faro nodded and Thomas continued, 'One reason for using Andy Carling as a messenger could have been a letter or something too important to be trusted to the mail.'

But Faro's mind was elsewhere. To him perhaps not the most important, but certainly the most worrying of all, was the question: Where did Lachlan Brown fit into these mysterious deaths?

Was the visit of the beggarman (alias Mr Glen alias Davy McNair) to the Assembly Rooms to warn the young pianist? And was the misjudged rifle shot coincidence or part of a sinister plot?

Requesting to be put off at his home in Sheridan Place, he gave Thomas certain instructions. As they sat outside the door the constable showed no inclination to leave and proceeded to go over the events of the last hour.

At last the front door of number 9 opened and Thomas leaned forward. His homely face lit up as the maid May walked down the steps with a shopping basket over her arm.

Stepping out of the carriage, he greeted her and for the first time ever Faro saw her smile and realized that he was witnessing a romance in the making.

He realized now why the constable was so eager to be on the beat in the Newington area.

'There's no hurry to get back, Thomas. Take a couple of hours off, you've worked for them!'

Thomas beamed gratefully upon him. Even May smiled shyly and Faro felt inordinately proud of his new role as Cupid.

Leaving the police carriage later, Faro was in time to catch Lachlan as he was running down the front steps of the Caledonian Hotel into a waiting carriage.

He stopped and pointed in amazement to the jacket which Faro carried over his arm. 'Where did you get that?'

And inspecting the label, he confirmed that this was the garment he had given to the old man from Glen Gairn.

'I doubt if there is another like it in the whole of Edinburgh. But how did you come by it?' he added again and indicated the carriage. 'Look, I'm late already. I'm going to George Street. Jump in and we'll talk on the way.'

Taking a seat alongside, Faro told him that the man who had come to his dressing room was dead. Lachlan gave a shocked exclamation when

Faro added that his name was probably McNair.

'That's it! Now I remember. Davy McNair. Poor man, poor man. How dreadful. I realize he looked half starved. If only he had come to me earlier.'

Faro decided not to tell him that McNair had probably been murdered as he continued, 'Look, can I do anything to help?' He paused awkwardly. 'I mean about the funeral expenses and so forth.'

'That's very good of you, sir.'

'Lachlan — please, Mr Faro.'

'Very well. I would be greatly obliged if you could find out anything about him as soon as possible — from Mr Brown — your uncle —'

Lachlan laughed. 'Well, that's easy. It so happens that Uncle John is going down to Osborne to join Her Majesty there. Knowing I was still in Edinburgh he decided to come to my recital tonight, to hear my new composition — incognito, of course. You understand!'

He paused. 'Look, why don't you have a word with him yourself? I'm sure he'll be glad to see you again after all these years.'

Chapter Nine

John Brown and Faro met that evening in Lachlan's dressing room at the end of his recital. Faro had not been present but was aware that Brown's appearance had created a mighty stir in the streets of Edinburgh, a sensation worthy of confirmation by the newspapers next morning: 'Famous young concert pianist meets his illustrious relative.'

Obviously John Brown had not the least idea what the word 'incognito' meant since he arrived by open carriage in full Highland dress. His red hair, beard and the 'Balmoral' bonnet identified him immediately to all of Edinburgh familiar with the *Illustrated News*, as well as those who had seen scurrilous cartoons and drawings of John Brown with Her Majesty circulated privately.

Faro and Brown were of equal height and, Lachlan decided, both somewhat intimidating personalities. Two men, he thought, suppressing a smile, who were more than a match for one another.

Faro, sensitive to atmosphere, was immediately aware that Brown, an indifferent actor, was not pleased by this unexpected encounter despite Lachlan's enthusiastic introduction. After a polite exchange of greetings and an acknowledgement of their last meeting, Brown surveyed the Chief Inspector from under lowered brows. His expression was one of extreme caution, his tone evasive, his words slow and chosen with care.

It was, thought Faro, as if he expected each one might be taken down and used in evidence. Not until much later did he realize the excellent reason for Brown's behaviour.

Unaware of any tensions between the two men, Lachlan said, 'I have told Uncle John about McNair's visit and that you would like to know more about his background.'

'I understand the puir man is dead,' said Brown.

'That is what we are investigating.'

The word 'investigating' startled Brown. He sat upright, listening carefully as Faro explained the circumstances of McNair's death.

'Do you suspect foul play?' he demanded sharply.

'That may be difficult to prove.'

Brown looked relieved and ceased chewing the end of his moustache as Faro added, 'However, unless his body can be formally identified and claimed within a few days, it must be disposed of by the city's medical officers.'

Brown nodded. 'I ken Davy McNair well. An awfae' like thing to happen to him. He was groom at Balmoral, been in Royal service as long as I can remember.'

'Had he any family?'

'He wasna' married, if that's what you mean. There was a sister, Bessie — twin to him. She was a housemaid at the Castle too and they had a cottage on the estate. They were near neighbours to your auntie.'

Listening, Faro felt triumphant. So his memory had not failed him entirely. He had doubtless seen Bessie McNair on his last visit to Deeside several years ago, for his aunt's birthday party begun in such high spirits and culminating in the mists of Glen Muick where only seconds separated the Queen from death at the hands of an assassin.

'When did they leave Her Majesty's service?'

Brown frowned. 'A while since. There was a wee bit of trouble.' He wriggled uncomfortably. 'I dinna ken exactly what was involved. Some sort of pilfering.'

'Pilfering? After many years of loyal service, that does seem a little strange.'

'Temptation, man. It's a great thing is temptation.' The deep sigh that accompanied his words indicated more clearly than any speech that this was a subject on which John Brown could say a great deal, indeed that he might prove to be something of an authority on temptations.

'I'll take a look, identify him formally, if ye like. He'd want to be buried in Crathie and I can arrange that. Any sign of his sister?' Brown added. 'Rumour had it she'd gone to Edinburgh. Mebbe he'd come to look for her.'

Faro did not relish having to tell that Bessie McNair was also dead, killed in a road accident.

Brown tut-tutted. 'Is that a fact now? Man, man, that's terrible. Although it's mebbe better that way. I mean them being so close. I've often heard tell that with twins, one doesnae' long survive the other.'

Reading Faro's doubtful expression, he said hastily, 'You're no' hinting that these unfortunate happenings were anything else but accidental, Inspector? A rare coincidence —'

A lifetime's association of dealing with highly suspect alibis had left Faro with no great faith in amazing or rare coincidences. The most amazing, he had found, were frequently the result of human agency.

Brown sighed. 'I can pay my last respects to Bessie too, then. Arrange a decent burial for them both. Someone'll need to do it, them having no kin.'

As Faro thanked him, he said, 'Just a matter of decency, man. Common decency, that's all.'

But as they parted, Faro decided that the swift change in Brown's manner from wariness to eagerness to be accommodating was a matter to give pause for thought. It was an attitude with which he was sadly familiar.

In anyone less important, such behaviour would have indicated the workings of uneasy conscience. And his interview with Brown served only to confirm the identities of the dead man and woman. He was no further forward in the matter of solving the mystery of the two deaths, which were being written off by the Procurator Fiscal as unfortunate accidents.

Superintendent McIntosh's attitude was unsympathetic. Within a year of retirement and nursing secret dreams of a knighthood, he was determined that the Central Office should present a good clean tidy appearance to his successor. Most important of all, it should be seen that Edinburgh City Police had an amazing record where violent crimes were concerned. He was anxious to portray Edinburgh as a safe city where men and women could go about their business in a kind of urban paradise: God fearing, true to Queen and country.

'Will you never give up, Faro,' he sighed wearily, 'and accept accidents without wasting your time and mine searching for some sinister motive? Can't you content yourself with the minor crimes that plague us? There's plenty of fraud and burglaries and crim. cons. that you could get your teeth into if you are ever out of a job.'

Faro was mortally offended at such a suggestion. 'Crim. con.', or 'criminal conversation', was the law's quaint description of adultery. It was also the kind of investigation he considered beneath the attentions of a detective who had dedicated his whole career to murder investigations.

Vince was more understanding. He knew his stepfather of old and, listening patiently as he had done so often in the past, reminded him gently, 'McIntosh is right, you know. It isn't anything to do with you really —'

'Wait a moment. Two murders in Edinburgh and nothing to do with me,' Faro exploded. 'If

81

that isn't my business, then I don't know what is!'

'Look, Stepfather. If John Brown and Balmoral are involved, thieving servants and so forth, then it is the business of the Aberdeen branch to sort it out. You know that perfectly well and you can be sure they already have it in hand.'

Pausing, he placed his fingertips together and regarded Faro over them, once more the doctor whose soothing manner was meant to inspire confidence in a particularly stubborn patient.

'From what you've told me, one thing is puzzling. Why did brother and sister live apart, when she already had a rented cottage in Duddingston?'

'Exactly what Constable Thomas observed!' said Faro. 'The answer is fairly obvious, lad. They had information so dangerous it was vital there was no connection between them.'

Vince considered for a moment. 'Blackmail, do you think?'

'Before I can answer that, I'd like a lot more details, particularly about that pilfering Brown mentioned.'

'If it was jewels, something of that sort, McNair's remaining in his sordid lodging could have indicated that he was trying to contact a fence,' said Vince.

'We have no idea of what was taken. Brown was very vague. All we know is that it was of sufficient importance to have cost two people their lives. So far,' Faro added grimly.

'About Bessie McNair's Irish visitors. Could it

be that the Fenians are busy again?'

Faro nodded. 'That thought had crossed my mind. Although they could have been innocent enough. There's plenty of Irish folk in Edinburgh.'

'And they don't fit the description of your two attackers on the Mound,' said Vince. 'As for a tall, slim woman concealing a pretty face under a veiled bonnet. It could fit almost any well-off Irishwoman living here.'

As he spoke he watched his stepfather's expression change. He hadn't the heart to suggest what was in the forefront of his mind: someone like Imogen Crowe, the Irish writer they had encountered during one of Faro's earlier cases on the Borders at Elrigg Castle.

He guessed that Faro had been a little in love with her. She was to get in touch with him when her travels brought her back to Edinburgh. But when time passed without any letters or communication, Vince presumed that Faro had dismissed her from his mind as she had apparently dismissed him from hers.

Oddly enough, it was Olivia who had brought it all back to Vince. Just a week ago she had been shopping with the maid May and was certain she had seen Imogen.

'Imogen or someone very like her, sitting in Princes Street Gardens. I was tempted to go for a closer look, but she was obviously waiting for someone and as I was trying to make up my mind, a young man came along and greeted her. He sat beside her and took her hand. They were obviously well acquainted. So I turned May round, made some excuse and hurried in the opposite direction.'

'Why on earth —'

'My dear, I simply didn't want to intrude. How embarrassing, especially if she wasn't Imogen or worse, was — and didn't remember me!'

'But you were friends, for heaven's sake.'

Olivia sighed. 'We did exchange a letter or two after Elrigg. I liked her very much, I even read her books and told her how much I enjoyed them —'

As Vince listened he thought that Imogen had perhaps written back only in politeness, answering a fan letter. But tactfully he refrained from mentioning it. Not for the world would he disillusion his darling Olivia.

'I sent her an invitation to our wedding, which she never even acknowledged.' Olivia sighed. 'Such a shame. The perfect opportunity for her to be reunited with your stepfather. I was vexed they hadn't kept in touch after Elrigg.'

'You are a wicked little matchmaker,' said Vince, smiling at her tenderly.

'I know,' she laughed shamelessly. 'But I do wish — and you know it would be a good thing — if the dear man remarried. All those good looks, that kind heart, going to waste.'

'He'd hate to hear you saying that about him. It's not how he sees himself at all. Anyway, Livvy, I don't think marriage is for him. He's married already — to the City Police. If only you knew how he reproached himself for neglecting my mother —'

'That was quite a long time ago,' Olivia reminded him. 'And it wouldn't have saved her life, poor soul. After all, she didn't exactly die of his neglect, having his baby.'

Now remembering Olivia's words and regarding his stepfather's remote expression, Vince quickly changed the subject to Rose and Lachlan Brown. He and Olivia had invited them to the Café Royale for lunch the previous day.

'We were sorry you couldn't be with us. It was quite an eye-opener. The two of them, I mean, quite besotted with each other I'd say.'

Faro's face clouded. The reason he had declined the invitation was precisely that. He dreaded seeing the young couple falling in love.

'There's definitely something in the air. Livvy's very good at spotting that sort of thing. I have learned that she's seldom wrong, so we can take her word for it.'

'Early days, surely?' Faro interposed. 'After two or three meetings.'

Watching him solemnly, Vince said, 'You don't look as if you welcome this new suitor, Stepfather.'

Faro did not reply, his expression enigmatic. Vince sighed. 'I'll be frank with you, I thought the idea was always that she should also forgo and forget Danny.'

Again Faro was silent and Vince continued cautiously, 'Any further developments there that we don't know about?'

'Rose doesn't talk about him,' Faro admitted reluctantly. 'It's the one point of disharmony between us. She knows that I cannot conceal my feelings about this relationship, the nearest we have ever come to a quarrel. So now his name is never mentioned on her visits.'

Vince shook his head. 'So you are both being quite ostrich-like about the whole thing. That's not always a good sign.'

Personally he could not understand what his stepfather had against Danny. He had always liked the young policeman. True, he was Irish and a Catholic, but Vince knew that was not the real reason for Faro's opposition.

Right from the beginning, although Faro would have been the first to praise McQuinn as a policeman and a splendid, reliable colleague, Vince guessed that he had never considered him good enough for his daughter.

Now Vince was puzzled by the fact that Lachlan, who was eminently suitable, a famous concert pianist, young, handsome, a composer with a great future ahead of him, should meet a similar reaction.

Maybe his stepfather just didn't want his elder — and, he had to admit, his favourite — daughter to marry at all.

'If you had seen her with Lachlan, well, I'd make a pretty good guess that the signs indicate that she has outgrown her childish infatuation for

Danny McQuinn. I'd suggest that a few hints about Lachlan Brown might not come amiss.'

Faro looked at him quickly. Could it be that Vince was deliberately ignoring or had never known or never guessed his deeply personal reasons for disquiet?

Or the reason why he deliberately avoided spending time in Lachlan's company when Rose was with him, certain that he would not be able to contain his secret knowledge?

Chapter Ten

Faro realized with dismay that Rose's visit would soon be over. As always he was consumed with guilt at having spent so little time with her. For once this fact did not seem to trouble her. She had Olivia — and Lachlan, yes, Lachlan too.

Petted and spoilt by Mrs Brook, she touched her slender waist and groaned. 'A few more days is all I can afford — I don't know how the people in this house can keep their figures intact with dear Mrs B's cooking.'

She had just returned from one of Olivia's charitable sales of work in Duddingston. 'I wish you could have seen it. It was as well we took May with us to help carry round all the things Olivia bought. We shall have enough antimacassars to furnish a regiment.'

Faro only half listened to the conversation around the table as a jar of Gentleman's Relish was put before him.

'I only went because I had promised two of my pupils I'd look up their great-aunts who live there. Thank goodness they were very much in evidence in the tombola department. They had met May before — it's a small world,' she said, smiling across at her sister-in-law.

Olivia was oddly silent, she had eaten little and was looking pale.

'I hope you're not overdoing it,' Vince whispered, taking her hand.

'Oh, hush, Vince.'

Rose turned excitedly. 'Livvy — is it — I mean, are you —'

Olivia smiled wanly. 'Well, you might as well all know. It's early days and I would rather have waited a little longer —'

'Come, my dear, you have a doctor for a husband after all,' said Vince, grinning broadly as he looked round the table. 'We have reason to believe that we will be proud parents come Christmas.'

Rose squealed with delight and hugged them both. Everything else was forgotten in the joy that greeted their news. Faro was particularly delighted as he had been hoping for such an announcement since, two weeks earlier, he'd discovered Olivia looking distinctly unwell and refusing the Sunday roast on the one occasion each week when all three shared a midday meal together.

'Things are changing in Sheridan Place, our numbers growing,' said Rose happily. 'Though I wouldn't bank on Olivia having May much longer. Romance is in the air,' she added mysteriously.

'You mean Constable Thomas,' said Faro.

'I might have guessed you knew about that too,' said Rose. 'I don't think Mrs Brook will grieve to see her go, although she will certainly need extra help. Isn't it exciting, Pa?'

'It's great news,' said Faro. 'I hope a new baby will mean we'll see you more often.'

'Often as I can,' said Rose vaguely. 'Depends on a lot of things.'

In the silence that followed it was his chance to ask about Danny and he let it go.

The following day Rose went to Lachlan's final concert, which coincided with her return to Glasgow. Lachlan's tour had been a tremendous success. Edinburgh had indeed welcomed him with open arms, every performance had been sold out, leaving Faro to ponder whether the warm reception owed as much to the notoriety of his connection with John Brown as the young pianist's undeniable talent.

It was with some disquiet that he learned from Rose that Lachlan had a free week before returning to London to prepare for a tour of European cities.

'He is coming to Glasgow,' she said dreamily.

'You'll be teaching, of course,' said Faro.

'The girls are on holiday next week — fortunately.' She laughed. 'So we'll have the days together at least.'

Realizing how deeply they were attracted and aware of the power and passion of love, Faro dreaded what might happen away from the restraining influence of Sheridan Place.

If only they could still talk together as they had done in the old days. As for McQuinn, she seemed to have forgotten his very existence. How that would have pleased Faro once upon a time and he was again reminded that one should take great care in what one asked the gods to grant, as they might well answer but in a manner quite unacceptable to the petitioner.

Fate, however, was on his side momentarily. Vince was summoned to the Caledonian Hotel in the early hours of the morning.

Lachlan had succumbed to the dreaded influenza which Vince and many other Edinburgh doctors suspected might reach epidemic proportions.

But Lachlan had youth and good health on his side. Vince decided to isolate him and hired a reliable nurse to take care of him.

'He should be fit to travel to London next week as planned,' Vince reassured them. 'But any ideas he might have had about going to Glasgow are definitely to be abandoned.'

Vince's stern instructions had made Lachlan groan but he felt too miserable and ill to do more than weakly protest.

When Rose was informed she immediately returned to Edinburgh prepared to take over the nursing herself if necessary. But Vince strongly opposed any such ideas.

'Influenza is not to be taken lightly. It is highly contagious,' Vince told her sternly. 'Besides, Lachlan is too poorly to receive visitors who will merely exhaust him and delay his recovery.'

Lachlan was not too ill to realize the dangers and absolutely to forbid Rose to come anywhere near him. He also had a young man's pride. The mirror held up for his shaving revealed that he looked far from the handsome, strong, virile man Rose was used to meeting and he disliked being seen when not at his best, especially by this woman he loved.

And so Rose had to be content to walk with her father on Arthur's Seat. It was an afternoon of soft sunshine dappling the hills, the gorse was now in bloom, the horizons stretching endlessly to where the River Forth joined the North Sea and was lost in shimmering haze.

They sat down together on a boulder and, leaning her head on his shoulder, Rose sighed comfortably.

'What a glorious day, Papa. We never have enough time together.'

He hugged her to his side. 'We never did have, lass. As you've grown up I regret more than anything that I lost so much of both my bairns' childhood.' He sighed heavily. 'Was I wrong not to keep you both here with me in Edinburgh after your mother died?'

She looked at him. 'I think Emmy and I always hoped that you might. We longed for the holidays and we used to count the weeks, striking them off the calendar. We always had such plans for where were going — with our Papa —'

And Faro remembered guiltily how often he had been unavailable on those visits, working on a case. Absorbed with some crime or other and only vaguely aware of his daughters' reproachful sighs, their need for him. Pretending not to notice how disappointed they were to be put in the charge of Mrs Brook, with all their splendid plans for him set at naught.

Dear, kind, good Mrs Brook, whose idea of entertaining children was giving them huge meals, filling the empty corners of their lives with loads of cakes and scones. But these two girls needed more than banquets to compensate for their ever absent father. Sadly he knew all too well that they would not have complained at plain bread and porridge if they could have shared it with him each day.

'I thought it was for the best, and that you were happy with Grandma in Orkney,' he said bleakly.

'We were, but we always hoped things would change.' After a moment she added slyly, 'We hoped that you might marry again. We used to say in our prayers, "And send Papa a good wife." '

Faro was taken aback by this confession. 'I thought little girls objected to wicked stepmothers.'

She laughed. 'Well, we knew we could rely on you to make a good choice. Life is such a great adventure, isn't it? Full of the unexpected.'

Looking at her smiling face, dreamy-eyed, staring over towards the coast of East Lothian where the prehistoric hillfort of Taprain dominated the horizon, Faro took a deep breath.

'The unexpected? Are we to presume that includes Lachlan?'

She turned, smiling at him. 'He is such a delight, isn't he? Imagine Inga St Ola being his mother and not able to keep him with her in Orkney, having to leave him with the Browns to grow up on Deeside. Life is very cruel.' She sighed and shook her head. 'Strange that I already feel as if I had known him all my life. That he has always been there, just around the corner, waiting.'

She turned to Faro for help, for confirmation and when he remained silent she continued, 'That sense of familiarity, almost of kinship — as if long ago we had met before. And I keep trying to remember when — where —' She shook her head. 'It's like a half-remembered dream.'

Again she looked at her father, appealing for what he had once been able to give her, assurances that they both felt exactly the same about life in general and personal relationships in particular. But his closed-in expression defeated her.

'Silly, isn't it?' she said lightly.

Faro could think of no reply. His heart failed him as he listened to the dreaded word 'kinship'.

'Are you going to see him again? I mean, once he returns to London.'

She turned to him. 'Of course we plan to meet. And we will write letters.'

Again his guarded expression worried her. 'Don't you approve of Lachlan?' she asked gently. And when he didn't respond with the affirmation she wanted, she said crossly, 'I don't understand how anyone — anyone in this world,' she repeated in exasperation, 'could disapprove of him.

94

He's so good and kind — and modest, although he's so clever and talented —'

Faro put an arm around her shoulders, kissed her cheek. 'I'm just a little bewildered by the suddenness of all this, lass.' He paused before adding gently, 'Once before when we had this sort of chat together, it was about Danny McQuinn, remember.'

'And you didn't approve of him either,' she said sharply. Then, with a sigh, she shaded her eyes and looked across at the gleaming estuary. 'Last time and the times before that, Danny was never mentioned between us and you know full well the reason why.'

Removing his arm from around her, Faro said, 'May I be permitted, as your father, then to bring up the subject again? Are you prepared to tell me honestly what are your present intentions regarding Danny McQuinn?'

Rose sighed deeply. 'Danny wants to marry me. I think you know or must have guessed that. It was the reason I took a teaching post in Glasgow. However, there is one impediment —'

'He's Catholic?'

She shook her head. 'I would never let religion stand between us. We have always said it wouldn't.' Again she sighed. 'You see, Danny wants to go to America. Emigrate. There are McQuinns over there who went after the famine and they've settled in Ohio and done rather well for themselves. One is a priest and the other a sheriff. They keep writing to Danny that America is the land of opportunity. Danny agrees. He knows he'll have to wait years and years for promotion to Chief Inspector. So he is seriously considering going.'

She paused. 'Naturally, he wants me to go with him.'

Faro could think of no reply to alleviate the agony of the great shaft that had been driven into the region of his heart. Rose, his beloved Rose, whom he now could see so regularly since she came to Glasgow, whose life he expected once again to run parallel to his own as it had done before Lizzie died. And now she was threatening to go and live in another country. Another continent. As far as Faro was concerned it might as well have been another planet.

Panic seized him. He might never see her again.

At last he summoned up words that sounded like lead. 'And have you decided?'

She thought for a moment. 'I have given it great thought, Papa. You must know that. I've loved Danny since I was twelve years old. I've never thought of marrying anyone but him. But — and it's a big but — I don't want to live in America. I'm not like Danny, I'm not ambitious and I haven't scores of relatives.'

She took his hand, held it tightly. 'I have only Emmy, who is going to stay in Orkney. And Gran — who's getting old and frail. There's Vince of course — and Livvy. But you're my Pa, you're special,' she added in a whisper. 'Besides I'm not the stuff pioneers are made of. I want to be with my people, with my family. With you.'

Leaning over she kissed his cheek. 'I want to know that you'll always be somewhere near me. I've promised to give Danny my answer, my decision, before he goes.'

'When is that?'

'Soon,' she said sadly. 'We decided that we must have time away from each other so that we could be sure. And when I came here last week, I thought then that I would be going back with my heart saying follow him, wherever he went — that he was my whole life. Now I'm not so sure.'

She smiled wanly. 'As I've said, life is such a great adventure and I've realized that I don't need to go to America to experience it.'

'Does Lachlan have a role to play in this great adventure?' he asked gently.

She laughed. 'I do most earnestly hope so, Papa. We have so much in common, he's opened up a new exciting world for me —'

Faro felt as if he was going from one agony to another even more bitter. Terrible as it was to lose Rose to America, perhaps never to see her again, but worse, far worse, was the blow he must deal her new-found happiness with Lachlan Brown.

How he might destroy his daughter's happiness for ever. Cowardice was not among Faro's vices. He was a brave man used to facing deadly foes, but today he felt no longer strong and resourceful. He felt odd and lost and he wanted this moment with Rose to last for ever with church bells echoing across Arthur's Seat from the city below. If only he could freeze time so that he — and she — might never have to walk down the hill and face the bitter truth that lay ahead.

Silently, he walked back with her to Sheridan Place, where one of Mrs Brook's special meals awaited their return.

Rose skipped at his side, her arm in his, smiling up into his face, happy and relieved that the barriers between herself and her dear Papa were down at last. Totally unaware of his preoccupation, she added to his misery with girlish confidences and hopes about Lachlan, Lachlan who had already promised to turn her dreams into reality.

Faro sighed. For once he was glad to find Constable Thomas on the doorstep, flirting gently with May who immediately disappeared indoors.

Thomas waited until Rose went into the house, then said: 'I have a message, sir, Superintendent's respects for interrupting your Sunday but there's a visitor he thought you should meet.'

'A visitor. Couldn't that have waited until tomorrow?'

'Apparently not, sir. I never saw the gentleman, but the urgency makes me think it's something to do with that pair in the mortuary —'

And Faro turned away from his own door almost with relief to the investigation of two murders still unsolved.

Chapter Eleven

In Superintendent McIntosh's office, Faro found Inspector Brewer of the Aberdeen City Police waiting to greet him.

Profuse in apologies for bringing Faro from his fireside on a Sunday evening, he said, 'Tomorrow would have sufficed, but I'm on my way to my niece's wedding in North Berwick.'

'Inspector Brewer thought it would be a good idea to establish contact in view of the Balmoral connection,' said McIntosh. 'Seeing that you both have had much experience in dealing with Royalty.'

Brewer eyed the Superintendent in the manner of one who would prefer to make his own explanations. 'Thank you, sir.'

He turned to Faro who was wondering what all this was about and finding it hard to suppress a growing certainty of trouble ahead, especially when Brewer added, 'I wonder if we might adjourn to my hotel.'

McIntosh was included in the invitation as a polite afterthought offered with so little enthusiasm that the Superintendent declined, hardly needing the excuse that, alas, Mrs McIntosh was entertaining friends to supper.

The Royal British Hotel overlooked Princes Street Gardens and, comfortably ensconced with a dram between them, Brewer came quickly to what Faro had already guessed was the reason for this meeting.

'This unfortunate business of two Balmoral servants being found dead. Her Majesty is most upset.' He paused to smile encouragingly at Faro. 'You know how very important the least of her little flock is to her.'

Faro stared at him dismally. He never would have thought it from his visits to the Castle and rumours that had filtered through to him. 'I understand these two left under a cloud.'

Brewer pursed his lips. 'That is so, that is so. Most unfortunate. However, John Brown has stepped in nobly. Admirable fellow, Brown. Can always be relied upon. Made all the funeral arrangements, I understand, paying for their interment at Crathie out of his own pocket. No expenses spared,' he added, stifling a hearty laugh with a sombre frown. 'And a nice touch of sentiment, the brother and sister laid to rest together.'

And with all the clues to their deaths unresolved. A nice touch indeed, thought Faro as he listened to the eulogy on John Brown. During their meeting in Lachlan's dressing room all his instincts had told him something was going on that Brown was deuced anxious to keep hidden.

Brewer, however, was a much better actor. He had much more expertise in dealing with mayhem than the Queen's favourite ghillie.

'I understand the two servants were in trouble — pilfering, was it not?' said Faro innocently.

Brewer gave him an anguished glance. 'That is so. That is so. Bad business. Temptation, alas. Temptation is an unfortunate part of the human condition, even among the best of us.'

'So Mr Brown informed me,' said Faro drily.

'Oh, indeed.' Brewer's relief was short-lived as Faro added, 'What was it they stole?'

Brewer winced at the word. 'I understand — on the highest authority — that these were relatively unimportant documents, letters and so forth, which Her Majesty would like recovered. That's all we're at liberty to say,' he added, closing his lips firmly.

'Are you at liberty to say whether these, er, documents would be of value to some foreign power?'

Brewer stared at him. 'You've hit it on the head, Faro, by God, you have.' He paused. 'Not exactly foreign, unless you regard Ireland as such. I'm afraid we're up against Fenians again.'

It was well known that the Queen did not like Ireland. She regarded the Irish as 'peculiar rather treacherous people. The lower orders had never become reconciled to the English rule, which they hate! So different from the Scotch who are so loyal.'

As for Fenians, she had been the target of plots, both real and imagined, since 1867 when the first alarm was raised and Secretary General Grey hurried to Balmoral with a report from Manchester that the Fenians were after her. A month earlier, in September, five Fenians had attempted to rescue two of their countrymen from a police van and a British constable had been killed. General Grey was determined to surround Balmoral with troops. The Queen would have none of it. She believed in the loyalty and protection of her Highlanders and John Brown in particular.

The 'Manchester Martyrs' as they were called by the Irish, were duly captured and hanged. 'Horrid people,' the Queen wrote to her daughter. 'We shall have to hang some and it ought to have been done before, but it is dreadful to have to press for such a thing.' A deputation pleading for mercy was headed off by Grey and never reached her. However, on the day of their execution she wrote, 'Prayed for those poor men last night.'

Worse was to follow. An abortive rescue attempt at Clerkenwell Prison resulted in a seventy-foot wall being dynamited and many people injured. The alarm was again raised while the Queen was at Osborne and a telegram from Canada reported eighty Fenians heading for the Solent, where they would cast anchor and when she was driving in the peaceful woods in her pony chaise she would be snatched from John Brown and he would be murdered.

Stubborn as her statesmen knew her to be, she suspected that Grey was merely trying to force her out of seclusion. She refused to leave but accepted extra police, sentries, the Guards and warships off Osborne. 'Such a bore,' she sighed and when it was later reported that the whole expedition was a myth she decided other reports of risings 'must be exaggerated' and took the authorities to task for their credulity.

Even when her son Prince Alfred was shot and wounded by a bullet in his ribs at a public picnic in Australia (the Fenian reprisal for the Manchester executions), his mother stated that people who could shoot her son, entirely unconnected with politics or the Irish, were 'plain wicked'.

Faro knew to his cost how obstinate and immovable the Queen could be. In recent years he had been involved in protecting her, with considerable difficulty, from a very real assassination plot at Glen Muick, which almost ended in disaster for all of them.

But others apart from Fenians hated the Queen and he didn't believe a word of Brewer's vague 'letters and so forth'. Only state secrets redeemable at a price were important enough to involve blackmail and sudden death, he thought grimly, aware of the significance of Miss McNair's Irish visitors and the events of the night of her death, including the attack on himself, which had not been for motives of robbery.

Brewer meanwhile had pulled his chair forward and was regarding Faro in an official manner.

'But I am sure you have the case well in hand, sir. With your usual and, may I say, famous expertise. Just as a matter of interest, off the record, of course, I would be obliged if you could furnish me with any of the details of your investigation regarding these two unfortunate deaths.'

What a speech, thought Faro admiringly. What a command of official language, almost as if it had all been carefully rehearsed beforehand.

Brewer watched Faro take out his notebook. 'I was attacked on the night the woman McNair was abducted —'

'*You* were attacked,' Brewer interrupted. He had not expected that and obviously found Faro's statement a matter of surprise. 'You, Faro. How extraordinary.'

'Not really, sir. I was boarding a carriage and Miss McNair rushed up to me and asked for help — "they" — someone — was going to kill her. I just had time to see the two men before they felled me to the ground. The same two men who, I believe, later murdered McNair. They were not ordinary villains intent on robbery since I was not robbed and I suspect that neither of the victims was in possession of any items of value.'

'Shocking! Scandalous behaviour!' muttered Brewer sympathetically. 'I trust you were not badly hurt, sir.'

'Thanks to my inordinately thick skull. The McNairs were less fortunate.'

Brewer tut-tutted, then beamed on Faro. 'And I have the evidence of my own eyes that you are in perfect health again. Do go on with your story.'

So Faro told him how Miss McNair had apparently died, run over by a carriage which failed to stop in Dean Village, and that her injuries included a fractured skull caused by a blow to the back of her head.

He paused and Brewer nodded. 'Ah, the significance of a similar attack upon your person led you immediately to suspect foul play. And then, of course, her brother dying in his lodgings. A most unfortunate coincidence.'

'Hardly, sir. There was evidence that he had been similarly assaulted although he might have suffered a heart attack as a result. For some reason, presumably connected with the crime, he was living under the assumed name of Mr Glen.'

Brewer spread his hands wide. 'Most natural that you should with all your experience immediately suspect that criminal activities were involved. Pray continue,' he said, listening impassively to Faro's account of the fire in Bessie McNair's cottage and her Irish visitors.

'I dare say it will all be sorted out in time,' he sighed.

'Had it not been for Mr Brown's visit to his nephew here in Edinburgh —' Faro continued.

'Nephew?'

'Lachlan Brown, the concert pianist.'

'Oh. Oh, yes, indeed. His nephew.' Brewer's emphasis indicated that his thoughts lay with the more scandalous version. 'Do go on.'

'We might never have established the identity of either of the dead persons.'

'Quite providential. Trust Brown to see the right way of things.' Brewer listened to the clock striking eleven with the relief of a prisoner hearing the opening of his cell door.

He rose to his feet, smiling, but Faro was not

prepared to end the interview yet.

'One moment. Tell me, how did you come by all this information that the McNairs were in Edinburgh?'

Brewer's eyebrows raised dramatically. 'Ah, Faro, we have our own methods. You surely know that. But you are to be congratulated on your own extremely efficient methods.' And, placing a conspiratorial finger to his lips, 'I can say no more.'

But Faro was not to be fobbed off in this manner. If the missing documents were worthless, Brewer had gone to a great deal of trouble to have this meeting with the sole purpose, he did not doubt, of finding out how much was known to the Edinburgh Police and to himself in particular.

'John Brown, as you know, is close to Her Majesty. She was in something of a panic about it all,' Brewer went on. 'I can leave the rest to your imagination, I am sure.' Then, with a sigh, he took out his pocket watch, consulted it solemnly and added, 'I have various things to do in preparation for tomorrow and it is imperative that I have a good night's sleep. I sleep uncommon badly in hotels, alas. Any way I can help you, don't fail to get in touch.'

'There is something else I think you ought to know,' said Faro. 'There was an assassination attempt on Lachlan Brown. As he was leaving the Assembly Rooms late one night last week. A rifle shot from a passing carriage narrowly missed him.'

'What!' exclaimed Brewer. 'I was never informed about this.' His indignation sounded genuine enough. 'Does Brown know?'

'Unlikely, since Lachlan told me in strictest confidence.'

'And you did nothing about it!'

'I'm telling you that I was bound to abide by Lachlan's wishes. He refused to have it reported officially. The lad is somewhat sensitive about publicity regarding his Balmoral connection.'

'Quite, quite. But this unprovoked attack gives one food for thought, does it not?' Puffing out his cheeks, he frowned. 'I presume he did not imagine it — that he has some proof?'

'I think I can vouch for that. I have in my possession the rifle bullet which I removed from the lintel of the door. And I firmly believe that his attackers in the carriage might well be the same two we're looking for in connection with the McNair murders.'

'So you think Lachlan Brown might also be a target for the Fenians.' Brewer chewed at his underlip. 'I trust you are wrong, Faro. Surely no political assassin would wish to kill a concert pianist, especially one who has performed in Dublin.' He sighed deeply and shook his head. 'Now I really must leave you.' He held out his hand. 'Rest assured that with the McNairs laid to rest, the documents they stole are of no value. Be that as it may, authority — if you get my meaning — those in high places are anxious that they be recovered and destroyed — unread' — he emphasized the word — 'if they come into your hands.'

He sighed. 'As for these two servants' unfortunate deaths. They must be dismissed officially as accidents, pure coincidence, which you will agree so often happens in life.'

Again he smiled. 'Such a great pleasure to meet you. I trust there will be other happier occasions when we are both more at leisure to enjoy them. At least I am delighted that I have been able to allow you to close your file with an easy conscience on this distressing case. One mystery less to solve in your busy life, eh?' he added with a hearty laugh. 'I am sure you will appreciate that.'

As they walked into the reception hall Brewer yawned. 'Oh, please excuse me. I am extremely weary. I've had a long day and I have to be up and about at the crack of dawn tomorrow. Tell me, do you know how long it will take to reach North Berwick by train?'

Faro was well acquainted with the area and its railway system. As they walked through the hotel lobby he gave Brewer the relevant information.

At the front door, as they shook hands, Faro asked where the wedding was taking place.

'St Baldred's Church. At ten A.M. — devilish early for my taste —'

As Faro walked home to Newington along the Pleasance, he had plenty to keep his thoughts occupied. He would have given much to know why Brewer had considered it necessary to journey to Edinburgh to meet his opposite number and instruct him so carefully in the matter of the Queen's missing documents without revealing anything of their contents. Vital documents that must be destroyed unread intrigued him. And dangerous enough to have caused two deaths and two unsuccessful murder attempts — on Lachlan Brown and himself.

Whatever Brewer's real motive, it had little to do with a family wedding and whoever did his investigating in Aberdeen had let him down badly.

The genial inspector was in for a disappointment if he made the journey to North Berwick and presented himself at the church for ten o'clock on Monday morning.

St Baldred's had burnt down in a disastrous fire some ten months ago.

Chapter Twelve

As Faro entered his own front door he was relieved to find Vince alone. Olivia had retired for the night and, as the two men shared a dram together, Vince was curious to hear the result of his stepfather's urgent summons to the Central Office.

He listened impassively to the new information provided by Inspector Brewer before asking, 'You think there is some possibility that the McNairs could have been recruited as Fenian agents?'

'I think that highly unlikely. According to Aunt Bella's Balmoral informants, all the tenants were known for their unswerving loyalty and discretion. Many were sons and daughters of the original servants who had served Prince Albert and the Queen when the Castle was first built.

'As for the lower echelons, they seldom cast eyes on members of the Royal family anyway, especially chambermaids with stern instructions that upon the Queen's approach they must drop everything and melt immediately into cupboards conveniently provided in the corridors of the Royal apartments.'

'What about outdoor servants?' Vince asked.

'Same rules apply. Gardeners disappear behind hedges or keep their heads well down into the flowerbeds if they happen to be on their knees already. As for stable hands holding horses' heads, they are instructed to avoid the eye-to-eye contact as they elevate Royal posteriors into the saddle.'

Vince chuckled. 'Complete nonsense, isn't it!' He thought for a moment. 'Did Brewer give any indication as to the information in these papers?'

'Only that they are of great interest to the Fenians.'

Vince frowned. 'Could there be secret negotiations concerning Irish Home Rule that the Queen has had forwarded to Balmoral? Is the old lady getting careless, do you think?'

Before Faro could reply, he continued, 'But even if the McNairs had access to private papers and documents, would they have been able to make sense of the contents and know they had something valuable in their hands? Even educated people have problems making sense out of official documents, as I know to my cost.'

'There you have it, lad. I was thinking the same thing. The McNairs realizing the value of what they had stolen is problematic. Aunt Bella told me that many of the lower servants were unable to read and write — in English. They speak the Gaelic and some have little education beyond the basic rudiments of counting their wages.'

'As I recall, Prince Albert was very keen to change all that. He even gave the tenants access to the Castle library,' said Vince.

'True, but with large families to provide for, tenants have always been proud and eager to seize the chance of putting their offspring to work at the Castle as early as possible.'

Vince nodded. 'And no questions asked presumably, a blind eye conveniently turned by the Master of the Household on a well-grown lad or lass of eight or nine who could pass for a twelve-year-old.'

Both men were silent for a moment, then as Vince refilled their glasses, Faro said grimly, 'It would seem that the McNairs had enough education to know about the contents of these letters or documents to get themselves murdered. And those Irish visitors at Miss McNair's cottage are a very sinister factor.'

'You suspect that the fire was started deliberately,' said Vince.

Faro sighed. 'I do. And, as far as I am concerned, I still have two murders to solve as well as an assault on my own person. Whatever is behind it all, Brewer, or someone in higher authority, decided it was worth his while coming to Edinburgh to warn me off —'

Vince did not find the story of the bogus wedding at St Baldred's amusing. He looked very concerned.

'I presume Brewer *is* Brewer?'

'Oh, no doubt about that. McIntosh's known him for years and has been quite voluble about his achievements.'

'What do you conclude then? Brewer is sent down to meet you on a fabricated excuse regarding the death of two Balmoral servants and state documents, which he now declares were relatively unimportant but if they happen to fall into your hands then they are to be destroyed — unread.' He shook his head. 'That doesn't make any sense at all.'

'It does to me, lad. I'm being warned off, that's what. Plain lied to. And, as I don't care to be taken for a fool, I shall proceed as if Brewer's visit never happened.'

'Hunt down the Fenians, you mean.'

'Exactly. They are lurking in the vicinity of Edinburgh, I'd swear to that. And as the evidence so far indicates that they haven't yet got possession of these documents, they are also in circulation somewhere.'

'All this is pure speculation, Stepfather, and as usual you can't do anything to prove or disprove it.'

Vince paused and added lightly, 'The only Irishwoman you ever encountered on a social level was that writer, Imogen Crowe.'

He could see by his stepfather's expression that he had touched a sore point.

Faro had hoped three years ago that she was sufficiently interested — even attracted — to him to keep in touch. But since the day they parted on the railway platform at Berwick Station, he had never heard from her.

True, he realized she was still writing books. In fact since their encounter at Elrigg he had held two of them in his hands in James Thin's Edinburgh bookshop. He had considered buying

113

them, and had abandoned the prospect. They would lie on the shelf unread, not only because his scant time for reading was devoted to Scott, Dickens, and his beloved Shakespeare, but because they were romances.

Love stories. And he was afraid of seeing himself in any of the characters, lampooned, caricatured.

Imogen Crowe possessed a sharp, unerring eye, always seeking out those weaknesses and flaws in a man's personality that were best hidden and he suspected she might portray him as a rejected lover, in a cruel or pitying light.

'Ever hear from her?' Vince asked casually.

'No. Why do you ask?'

'I wouldn't have brought up the subject, Stepfather, but Olivia and I thought we saw her at the theatre the other night. We were sure it was her. Livvy had seen her, or someone deuced like her, a couple of weeks ago sitting in Princes Street Gardens. However, if she saw us then she didn't want to be recognized.'

He smiled, trying to make it sound trivial, as he added, 'She was accompanied by a young man — about my age, or younger.'

Faro got the point. A young man twenty years his junior. So Imogen had found a lover. No matter, no matter, he told himself. But dreams told him otherwise as he pursued her across the heathery slopes of Arthur's Seat, held her to his heart and whispered, I love you, I love you.

He awoke feeling elated, certain that he was

going to see her again. They would meet quite by chance in the High Street and she would explain away his fears, give a reasonable and true explanation for her long silence.

The fickle character of dreams was soon made evident when at the Central Office the McNair case was closed, the Procurator Fiscal's ruling 'accidental death', and their bodies removed for burial at Crathie kirkyard.

John Brown had been good to his word. And so had Superintendent McIntosh.

He was awaiting Faro's arrival next morning, flourishing a paper in his hand. 'You're acquainted with this case about the break-ins at Stirling Castle, Faro. Well, the lads over there haven't made a deal of progress and they have appealed for your expertise —'

'On robberies, sir? Surely there are other officers —'

'Yes, yes. But you have the experience,' said McIntosh sternly. 'Right away, Faro, if you please,' he added, closing the door behind him.

Experience, no doubt, but Faro felt this was an excuse at Brewer's urgent instigation — or what he had called 'a higher authority' to divert Inspector Faro's energies into less troubled waters.

Chapter Thirteen

As the Highland train steamed along the line towards Stirling, Faro gazed out on the Trossachs, with Ben Lomond snow-capped still and shimmering in sunshine. On the wooded foothills there were glimpses of fleeing deer herds and, from tiny hamlets, children rushed out gleefully to wave to the passing train. Horse-drawn traps waited at level crossings and farmers led cattle homewards for milking while on grassy hills shepherds with dogs rounded up sheep panic-stricken by the steaming monster on the railway line below.

Faro sighed at these tantalizing glimpses of a world utterly desirable and now utterly alien to him. Suddenly he was wistful for this other life akin to his childhood in Orkney and so remote from the great city of Edinburgh he had chosen to live in.

How good it would be to step off the train and follow that tree-lined track up into the hills. If only a man were free to follow his dreams. And he realized how seldom the nature of his work with the Edinburgh City Police allowed him the luxury of a holiday. As one case closed there was always another awaiting him in the wings.

He sat back in his seat. Instead of rebelling at his temporary removal from Edinburgh, this time he would obey. Instead of damning McIntosh for extracting him from a murder investigation he would be grateful to him, grateful to the higher authority that had left him with two fewer murders to solve.

For once, he was going to enjoy himself.

The approach to Stirling was impressive. The Gateway to the Highlands, a Royal burgh and counry town, it was a place of considerable historic significance, the choice of the most obvious strategic site on what had been the principal ford of the River Forth for the ancients who had created the town always with defence at the forefront of their minds. They had built their Castle on an extinct volcano, akin to Edinburgh's Castle Rock and the Bass Rock, with a similarly commanding position over the landscape.

In medieval days it had controlled the main north route through Strathallan to Perth, a convenient and vital base from which to show the Royal flag in central Scotland.

With a day in hand before this early meeting with the Stirling Police, Faro decided to climb the steep hill up to the Castle and explore at first hand its Royal historic connections.

Alexander I had died within its walls in 1124. A few years later King David I referred to his 'burgh of Stirling', already a place of some importance, long before two of Scotland's greatest battles were fought in the neighbourhood.

The original site of Stirling Bridge had changed

long ago but the decisive battle where the great William Wallace trapped and routed the English army under the Earl of Surrey in 1297 had gone down in history, as had Robert the Bruce's defeat of Edward II at Bannockburn in 1314.

A turbulent existence led to relative peace under James I a century later when the town expanded and the Castle became a popular Royal residence for the Stuart Kings. Here James II was born and his son James III enthusiastically made architectural improvements. Here Mary Queen of Scots was crowned as an infant after the death of her father James V at Falkland. Here her son James VI, and I of England, was both christened and crowned. In his turn he had the Chapel Royal rebuilt for the christening of his son Prince Henry.

The town of Stirling, like Edinburgh, was recognizably divided into old and new, thought Faro, the suburbs stretching out like groping fingers to a modern residential district for its affluent citizens.

In search of suitable lodging near the Castle he walked down the cobbled steep approach to Castle Wynd, St John and Spittal Streets. Like Edinburgh's High Street they contained good surviving domestic buildings dating from the sixteenth century: Argyll's Lodging, Mar's Wark and the handsome Guildhall, which was the centre of government.

The exterior of an attractive tavern appealed to him. This would best serve his purpose. A pleasant comfortable room and the excellent supper he was served confirmed the wisdom of his choice and he retired that evening well fed with every care firmly banished from his mind.

Next morning he presented himself at the local police station and was duly transported to the Castle by an earnest sergeant with a sheaf of papers relating to the break-ins.

Faro examined the scene, read through the documents with their interviews of the suspects of which the sergeant was inordinately proud. The evidence was laid before him by the sergeant in a most efficient manner, and they both agreed on the vital clue that established the criminal's identity. All that remained was an arrest and trial, neither of which need concern Faro personally.

Returning to the little tavern he also decided that his journey had been a waste of the Central Office's time, confirming his suspicions that it was a conspiracy between McIntosh and Brewer to distract his attention from the McNair murders.

Once the thought would have angered him; now it suited his purpose to humour his Superintendent by obeying orders, grateful to the circumstances, however dubious, that had removed him from the contemplation of violent crime. Let someone else enjoy the headache of sorting out whatever machinations were emanating from Balmoral Castle under the stage-management of the Queen, ably assisted, he did not doubt, by John

Brown's advice and counsel.

He would remain in Stirling until the criminal was charged at the end of the week, regard this as a well-earned rest and, taking advantage of the mild, sunny weather, indulge in his once-favourite pursuit of exploring local beauty spots and historic monuments.

And remembering Vince's sage advice about crossing bridges before he came to them, he also deliberately thrust Lachlan and Rose from his mind. Lachlan had not asked Rose to marry him and, until he did so, there was no reason for Faro to take any action.

As for Fenians — he hoped he had heard the last of that dreaded word in this peaceful town.

His hopes were short-lived.

An item in the daily newspaper indicated that in Stirling, at least, they were at large.

A young newspaperman was in custody, charged with Fenian sympathies and subversive behaviour.

His name was Seamus Crowe. It was the name that drew Faro's attention and as a heavy shower of rain had put paid to his plans to walk towards Flanders Moss, he decided to satisfy his curiosity by attending the nearby courthouse that morning.

Perhaps Crowe was a common enough Irish name, but the main reason for Faro's attendance was the hope that Crowe would be revealed as one of two men who had attacked him. It was a chance not to be missed; he would enjoy the satisfaction of seeing the man condemned and justice done. And at the back of his mind, revived once more, was the possibility of proving a link with the McNair murders.

He was to be disappointed. He listened to the charge. Seamus Crowe had been arrested for unruly behaviour, disturbing the peace and expressing seditious sentiments at the Mercat Cross. He was accused of expressing anti-Royalist sympathies and inciting the listeners to riot during a political meeting addressed by the distinguished Ulster Member of Parliament Sir Hamish Royston Blunt, who happened to be a Stirling gentleman with Royal connections.

Sir Hamish was also in court that day and Faro recognized the fine Highland features as well as the stir his presence created. He watched him listening intently as Crowe was charged with carrying a banner bearing the words 'Home Rule for Ireland. Erin Go Brach' (translated for the court as 'Ireland for Ever') and for confronting Sir Hamish and attempting to do him grievous bodily harm by assaulting him with the said banner.

Crowe interrupted at this point, shouting in protest that he had no intention of harming Sir Hamish, that he had merely thrust forward the banner for him to see the words.

He was silenced immediately and the court called to order.

Proceedings continued. Crowe had been restrained from approaching Sir Hamish by several town officers and, in the scuffle that followed, he had struck a constable across the mouth, thereby slackening one of the said constable's teeth.

From his seat in the gallery, Faro had lost interest in the case, bitterly disappointed that the prisoner Crowe, an earnest and delicate-looking young man with carrot-red hair and spectacles could not, by any stretch of imagination, have been one of the bullies who had attacked him. He hardly listened to the heavy sentence being passed on Crowe, a fine of several hundred pounds and six months in gaol.

With the sensitivity he had developed over the years, he was aware of being watched, of close scrutiny. Turning his head cautiously, his eyes met those of Imogen Crowe.

A moment later, she pushed her way towards the bench, thereby breaking all the rules as she shouted that the sentence was grossly unfair but that she was willing to put up bail for the young man who was her cousin and pay whatever costs were involved.

The Sheriff was not well pleased by this interruption or by the remotest possibility that Seamus Crowe should escape imprisonment. He demanded her name.

Kinship to the prisoner and Imogen's accent infuriated him further. A passionately religious Orangeman, he hated the Catholic Irish with a passion that included a regret that the practice of hanging, drawing and quartering all traitors, especially Irish traitors, was out of date by more than two hundred years.

Ignoring Imogen's offer, he took the opportunity to admonish her in the strongest possible terms for this unseemly interruption, informing her that he regarded the sentence on the young man as too lenient. Exclaiming against the effrontery of one Fenian defending another in a British court, he demanded to know by what rights this woman was not being charged for associating with a criminal movement.

'Is this to be the new path of British justice?' he appealed to the court in general and found to his delight a murmur of approval, a few loud 'Hear, hear's.

Worse was to follow. It so happened that the Sheriff was a keen reader and Imogen Crowe's banned book on life in a woman's prison in London had fallen into his hands. He was about to play his ace card: 'Can the prisoner be defended by a woman who had once served a term of imprisonment herself for Fenian activities?'

This was too much for Faro. He went forward, approached the bench and begging their indulgence announced himself as Chief Inspector Faro of the Edinburgh City Police. He was prepared personally to vouch for Miss Crowe. Regarding her book, he respectfully drew the Sheriff's attention to the fact that, since its publication, her innocence and wrongful imprisonment had been proved.

His name drew respect and so did his reputation. No one lightly tackled the sincerity or the findings of the distinguished detective.

123

The Sheriff gave Faro a venomous look and apologized obliquely to Miss Crowe but that was as far as he was prepared to go. Bail was refused for Seamus Crowe and, despite the protests, he was sent to gaol for six months.

Watching Crowe led away to the cells, Faro guessed that this was doubtless the young man Vince and Olivia had seen with Imogen in Edinburgh. That he was her cousin should have cheered him, except that the description of a young man with red hair and spectacles and a woman, tall, slim and veiled but pretty, also fitted the description of the mysterious Irish couple who had visited Miss McNair's cottage.

Faro left the court hastily with the unhappy thought that if his suspicions were correct, then Imogen and her relative were connected with the Fenians' involvement in the papers stolen from Balmoral. And that they were prepared to murder to acquire those documents.

He guessed that they had done so already and decided grimly that if all did not go according to their plans, the Fenians would be capable of further murders.

As for himself, it was less than consoling to his unblemished reputation that, by his action in supporting Imogen Crowe in court, he had undoubtedly assisted a miscarriage of British justice.

Chapter Fourteen

As Faro hovered indecisively outside the court, hoping that Imogen Crowe might appear, Sir Hamish hurried down the steps.

He was alone and, seeing Faro, bowed politely. 'You will not be offended if I tell you, sir, that I thoroughly applaud your action in defending that young woman. It fits in with all I have heard of your reputation for justice and fair play.'

Faro, somewhat embarrassed, murmured his gratitude. As they shook hands, he looked again at Sir Hamish. There was something familiar about him.

'Have we not met before, sir?'

Sir Hamish studied him intently for a moment and then shook his head. 'Not that I am aware of. Your name is well known to me in Scotland and I am sure I would not have forgotten meeting you.' He smiled. 'And it is a pleasure to do so now. Good day, Inspector.'

As Sir Hamish climbed into the waiting carriage, Faro again turned his attention to the court door. Should he wait for Imogen Crowe to emerge, or return to his lodging and avoid a meeting? He was not surprised to find that she still aroused emotions dormant in him. Emotions he decided that could be dangerous for them both.

Then he saw her, walking swiftly, gracefully,

eyes narrowed against the sunlight streaming into the doorway. The slight hesitation told him that she had seen him. She moved indecisively, a gesture indicating that she also wished to avoid this encounter. But was her reaction for the same reason, Faro wondered.

For one instant he thought she was going to turn on her heel, head in the opposite direction. He knew he could not let this happen, that he would always regret having let this moment pass.

'Imogen!'

She looked at him, smiled, managed to make it look as if she was surprised to see him waiting for her. She came forward, hand outstretched, and a drift of perfume reminded him of their first meeting at Elrigg. In retrospect it seemed impossible to believe that once he had so heartily disliked her.

'Thank you for your help. I'm in your debt, Inspector — as usual,' she added, her wry look showing that she too remembered.

'It's been a long time, Imogen. Three years.'

She shrugged. 'Nearer four.'

He felt a moment's joy. She had counted them more carefully than he had.

'I don't know where the years go to —'

Hardly a compelling or original statement, he thought, the usual excuse signalling either neglect, indifference, or both.

She ignored it and continued, 'Seamus will be grateful to you. He's a good lad, a bit impulsive. The dedicated patriot, but I dare say he may grow out of it some day. Anyway, it is good to see you again. You are looking well,' she added, trying in vain to sound genuinely interested.

He could think of nothing more to say. She hesitated a moment and then began to walk away from him. Her action, her small gesture of the head indicated that she had no wish to prolong this meeting or further their association beyond the bounds dictated by gratitude and politeness.

Desperately, he fell into step at her side.

'Where are you staying?'

'At the Golden Lion there.' She pointed. 'Convenient for the court.' She looked at him. 'Are you here on police business?'

'Yes. It was quite by accident I read about your nephew's trial.'

'Then we should both be grateful to you.'

They had almost reached the hotel.

'What are you doing now?' he asked.

'Still writing books. Still travelling.'

'Good. I meant for the rest of the day.' And when she shrugged, 'Shall we have lunch?'

'If you wish,' she said. Her voice, sad and tired, lacked enthusiasm.

He pretended not to notice. 'Splendid. Where shall we go?'

The hotel was an impressive building built in 1786. 'This will do. Food's good enough for the visiting judges and it boasts of being patronized by Royalty.'

Seated at a table overlooking the street, she looked up from the menu and said, 'I thought I

127

saw Olivia and Vince at the theatre one night when Seamus and I were in Edinburgh.'

'When was that?'

'A few weeks ago. I gather they are married now.'

'And have been for a couple of years.'

'Are they happy?'

'Very!' Faro looked at her wistful expression. What an odd question.

'I'm delighted. Do give them my best wishes,' she added with a smile and continued to study the menu.

Faro was pleased to notice from her order that her appetite was unaffected by the recent traumas of the court.

'Are you often in Edinburgh?'

'From time to time. When my writing takes me there.'

That promise when they last met to keep in touch was avoided and Faro had few memories of the food served to them, poor or excellent it would have made little difference. Not only did his appetite flag but so did the conversation deteriorate to a careful inconsequential chatter between strangers.

Faro looked at her bleakly. He felt that his presence bored her, and that she regretted having accepted his invitation. And all the while he was trying not to notice how attractive she was, with her soft Irish brogue, trying not to let his emotions be influenced by this charming exterior, while she regarded him from behind some impenetrable barrier she had deliberately raised between them.

At last the meal was over, the bill paid. She thanked him profusely, said how nice it had been, seeing him again, and how grateful she was. And Seamus too.

'What are you doing for the rest of the day?' he interrupted.

She stared at him wide-eyed, as if this was a completely unexpected and somewhat improper suggestion. Then she shrugged and laughed, a laugh soft and deep in her throat that he remembered.

'Not a great deal. At least not until evening. Then I must visit Seamus.'

'And after that?' he asked, hoping to sound casual and failing miserably to hide his eagerness.

Her eyes widened again momentarily before she looked away from him, studying the staircase as if it offered immediate escape from a difficult situation.

'I have other people to see. I intend to fight with every means possible against Seamus's sentence. So grossly unfair, it is.' Turning to him again, she said, 'Now, if you'll excuse me —'

Reluctant to let her go, he said desperately, 'What about tomorrow then?'

She shook her head but he pretended not to notice. 'Look, my official police business is finished. I don't need to go back until evening — catch the last train.'

She smiled and, suspecting hesitation, he seized her hands, held them tightly. 'Shall we spend the day together? Please, Imogen.'

The smile vanished. Her face expressionless, she said, 'That would be fine. Sure now, I would enjoy that.'

'See you after breakfast then.'

He watched her go. At the foot of the stairs she turned, faced him. For a moment he thought she was going to change her mind but, with a shrug, she ran lightly upstairs.

He slept badly that night. Vivid dreams concerning the following day awakened him like warning signals of evil to come. But worst of all was the knowledge his waking mind stubbornly refused to accept. How Seamus Crowe fitted exactly the description of one of the visitors to Miss McNair's cottage and it took little imagination to identify the veiled young woman as Imogen Crowe.

They were Irish with Fenian sympathies. And as the two people had been murdered, their connection, however vague, made them possible suspects whom Chief Inspector Faro in any other circumstances would have been very eager to question.

Chapter Fifteen

Arriving at Imogen's hotel in good time for their breakfast meeting, Faro asked the desk clerk if one of the pony chaises they advertised for the use of residents was available for hire.

The arrangement made, he hurried into the dining room. There was no sign of Imogen and in a pretence of reading the morning newspaper he sat through half an hour of despair.

She had changed her mind.

But as he was about to leave a message for her, she appeared breathless in the hall.

'Sorry about that. I had someone to see late last night. And I overslept.' She smiled. 'Sir Hamish has offered to put in a plea for Seamus, to have his sentence reduced. Isn't that wonderful? Especially when he's from the North —'

'He lives in Ulster, but he was born here in Stirling. He's a Scotsman,' Faro corrected her.

'He still belongs to those we are fighting against. But he's a very nice man.'

Faro had already decided that from his fleeting acquaintance outside the court with the man whose looks were so familiar.

'No, thank you,' said Imogen to his offer of breakfast. 'I'll keep my appetite. Were are we going?' she asked as he led her outside to where the pony chaise was waiting for them.

The sun shone radiantly, the streets gleaming after an early shower of rain.

Half an hour later they were trotting briskly along the road towards Menteith and Inchmahome. A boat was for hire and Faro rowed towards the island which beckoned over the water.

'How lovely,' said Imogen as they stepped ashore.

As they walked towards the ruined priory, Faro said, 'It has quite a history. Mary Queen of Scots stayed here as a child with her four Marys, safe from the machinations of the Scottish nobles. Here is the spot where they played, according to legend: Queen Mary's Bower.'

The sky clouded over and a thin breeze ruffled the waters. The feeling of rain was in the air and they took shelter in the crypt, burial place of the lairds of Menteith — lairds with their ladies, resting at their sides for all eternity, in that peaceful place.

The sun returned and they sat on the turf with their backs against a broken wall. 'I must thank you,' Imogen smiled and looked across at the priory, 'for such an unexpected — happy day, and this pretty place.'

'Perhaps we'll meet again — visit other magic places —'

She shook her head. 'No.' Her tone was firm.

'Why not?' he demanded sharply.

Turning, she looked at him, exploring his face with eyes that held a caress. 'You know the reasons perfectly well, I think, Inspector Faro,' she said softly.

'I thought we had agreed you were to call me by my name,' he reminded her gently.

'No. Inspector Faro will do fine for what I have to say. It is better for us both this way. Sure, I was glad to see you. Don't think for a moment that I'm forgetting what you did for my reputation, but friendship between us is not — and can never be — part of the deal.'

'Friendship is not precisely what I have in mind —'

She covered her ears, shook her head as if to thrust away his words.

Dragging her hands away, he held them firmly and said, 'Hear me out —'

She looked up at him. 'No, you hear me out. I am doubly grateful to you for giving me a character reference, let's not forget that. But — and it's a big but — there's two hundred years of bitterness and the Fenians between us.'

She gestured to the ruined walls of the priory. 'This is your history; mine is even older. We belong in the mists of legend, the pre-Christian Fenians — *fianna,* as they were called, were a band of warriors like those of King Arthur. It was an order of chivalry, the very spirit of Ireland, heroic conduct with magical undertones. The number of *fianna* was seven score and ten chiefs, every one having nine fighting men under him, and each of them bound by three sacred vows: to take no woman or goods by force, to refuse none who asked for cattle or bread and to fight to the death at the side of their chief. And no man was worthy to join the *fianna* till he knew by heart twelve books of poetry. Not even for the country of everlasting youth — the *Tir nan Og* — would the *fianna* give up Ireland —'

Faro listened silently, studying her face, observing in her eyes conviction and complete dedication to the Irish cause.

'The saga combined self-reliance, attachment to the earth and a strong ring of anti-clericism. The *fianna* flourished in Ireland in the second and third centuries of the Christian era. They resisted conversion and when St Patrick pronounced the doom of hell upon them for their pagan ways, the bard Oisin told him: "Better to be in Hell with Finn, than in Heaven with pale and flimsy angels . . ." '

Faro groaned inwardly. Her ringing tones, her shining eyes also pronounced doom on his growing love for this passionate patriot who was doubtless a member of a terrorist organization.

She turned on him and smiled. 'Even today, I believe their pagan beliefs are stronger than lip service to the Virgin Mary.'

'Such sentiments are splendid, Imogen, but they belong in legend. Frankly, I cannot reconcile chivalry with hearts that throw bombs to maim and destroy, and assassinate their political opponents in the name of religion.'

'Sure and I agree with you — in principle. But who first drew the sword in Ireland? Not the Irish,

134

I can assure you. We were a conquered race, like you here in Scotland. God knows, you people have even less to thank England for. We have Cromwell's murderers but you have Edward the Third at Flodden Field and Butcher Cumberland at Culloden. As for the name Fenian, it was chosen about a generation ago for the new embodiment of Irish national feeling. Not to be confused with the more modern Irish Republican Brotherhood of the last decade.'

'With its murderers,' he interrupted.

She paused apologetically. 'I didn't mean to give you a lecture, Inspector, but it's all very close to my heart. I grew up with the legends. The heroes were real people to me and my uncle, Seamus's father — him your people murdered —' she added bitterly, 'he made me learn them by heart. My childhood was steeped in the sagas. That's probably what made me a writer.' She sighed. 'Every day I had to recite a new passage and he made me promise to do the same for his son should anything happen to him —'

As she spoke Faro thought of her uncle Brendan Crowe, the fanatical patriot who had brought his adopted niece with him to London, his whole purpose to kill the English monarch whom he held personally responsible for all Ireland's sorrows, past and present. In an assassination attempt on the Queen in St James's Park, he had been fatally wounded by the police. Rather than be taken prisoner he shot himself in his lodging. Imogen, a girl of sixteen, was with him and, accused of sheltering a terrorist, she was sent to prison.

'You can't blame Seamus,' Imogen went on. 'He was born and bred to hate the English and die for Ireland. A passion and loyalty so strong he was even willing to leave his young wife and baby son back there, believing that as a newspaperman in Scotland he could do more to further the cause, certain that, with Home Rule just around the corner, he could recruit a few good fighters to scare the wits out of the British.' She made a wry face. 'And not only with guns. He claimed I had taught him that the pen was mightier than the sword.'

A shrill whistle announced the boatman's return and as they walked towards the landing-stage she took from her reticule a small booklet, hardly bigger than a pamphlet. 'Read this sometime. It will help to set your ideas right about the movement.'

With a gesture of impatience, Faro thrust it into his pocket, aware that for him the day was almost over. He was conscious that little had been achieved. Painfully aware that the vivid unhappiness of the dreams that had haunted him were on the way to realization, he looked sadly across at Imogen.

Ignoring him, she trailed a hand in the water and watched the island all the way back to the shore while Faro searched her face for regret. The regret he was feeling was that somehow they had left part of their lives, lived briefly in less than an hour, on that strangely magical island. He would hold in memory for ever Imogen clasping her knees as she sat on the velvet turf by the ruined wall, the breeze ruffling her dark hair, the vision of Inchmahome with its tombs of warriors, and the voice of Imogen Crowe reciting the story of the *fianna*.

In the pony chaise that awaited their return all such magic evaporated. Faro's mood changed to deepest melancholy, as a thin driving rain cut sharply across Flanders Moss and struggling to hold up an umbrella against the elements left little chance for conversation.

Outside the hotel, Imogen once more held out her hand.

'Goodbye — and thank you again.'

'Is it to be goodbye? Can we not make it *au revoir?*'

Stubbornly she shook her head. 'No. Goodbye it is.'

'Why, Imogen, why?'

'Sure, haven't you taken in a word of all I tried to tell you out there?' she demanded, shaking her head. 'There's the Irish Sea and two hundred years of bitterness between us, remember.'

'Seas can be sailed on; bitterness can be laid aside. Others than ourselves have overcome it in the past —'

'But not us, Inspector. Not us.'

Stirred by his bleak expression, she put a gentle hand on his arm. 'You are a dangerous man, Jeremy Faro.'

He laughed, pleased she had used his name. 'How dangerous?' he said putting a hand over hers. 'I am very gentle with those I love. With my friends.'

'I can never be your friend. I could only ever be your lover.'

His heart leapt at the word. 'That too, then, if you want it that way.'

She shrugged. 'There is no way for us. As well you know.'

'Why not?'

'Because it would destroy us both. I have my own path, my own destiny to follow, and it can never run parallel with yours.' She sighed impatiently. 'Sure, and I told you all this once before when we were at Elrigg.'

Astounded at his own audacity, his recklessness, he seized her arms, held her close. 'You could marry me,' he whispered.

She started back, looked at him, gave him the dear crooked smile he had learned in this short time to love and dread. 'Is it proposing you are, Jeremy Faro?' she asked softly.

'If you wish.'

She shrugged. 'If wishes were horses, beggars would ride,' she said gently and, coming towards him, she stood on tiptoe and kissed his cheek. 'Goodbye it is, my dear.'

And turning, tears suddenly threatening, she ran up the steps.

'Wait! Imogen — wait!'

He called in vain. He watched the door close, carrying her out of his life once more.

Her departure left him with several empty pain-ful hours to be endured before his train to Edin-burgh. For a while he lingered in the hotel in the hope that she might change her mind and bring him the happy ending all his senses craved.

Then, unable to wait patiently any longer but reluctant to relinquish the dream, he paid his bill and said that he would return for his luggage in an hour or so.

At the door, he returned to the desk. 'If anyone asks for me I am taking a walk across to the Beheading Stone.'

He was curious about the ancient landmark, scene of many gruesome executions in Stirling's history, and the sun was already falling from an azure sky towards a dark horizon as he trudged across the fields.

He sat down by the stone and took out the booklet Imogen had given him. As he expected, it concerned Ireland's great leaders and sad he-roes and this setting provided a suitable atmo-sphere of melancholy.

The political roots of Fenianism, he read, are to be found not in the legends of Finn and Oisin but in the rising of the United Irishmen in 1798 by Theobald Wolfe Tone who wrote: 'To break the connection with England, the never-failing source of all our political evils; and to assess the independence of my country — these are my objects. To unite the whole people of Ireland, to abolish the memory of past dissensions, and to substitute the common name of Irishmen in place of the denominations of Protestant, Catholic and Dissenter — these are my means . . .'

With a gesture of impatience Faro cast it aside. Damn them all. Damn the Fenians. If only Imogen Crowe had not been Irish they might have had a future together. Trust him to fall in love with a passionate patriotic Irishwoman — and a writer too.

Had anyone told him three years ago that this was what fate held in store he would have laughed them to scorn. And now here he was trapped by his own emotions with yet another love that could never be.

He shivered. It was cold and dismal by the stone with its grim history and sad ghosts. He wished he had stayed in the warm and welcoming parlour of the tavern with a dram at his side.

With a sigh, he consulted his watch. Time to go for the train and shake the dust of Stirling off his feet with its waste of the Edinburgh City Police's time and the bittersweet memory of his second encounter with Imogen Crowe.

Wearily he began to walk down the hill and, as he did so, he was aware of a closed carriage on the road below. It had stopped momentarily as if the coachman was unsure of his direction.

A moment later, the shrill whine of a rifle bullet had him face down in the heather. It was an instinctive movement that saved his life for a second shot ricocheted off a boulder close by. This was followed by the sound of a swiftly departing carriage and at last he felt safe to raise his head.

He looked around. There was no sign of game or animals in the vicinity and as he ran down the hill he knew that the target had been himself and he had narrowly escaped death.

Someone had tried to kill him.

And in much the same circumstances as Lachlan Brown on the night someone shot at him leaving the Assembly Rooms. There had to be a connection.

The road was deserted but he walked warily, fearfully keeping close to the hedgerows and fences, ready for instant action each time the sound of wheels approached from the direction of Stirling.

Carriages were few and none concerned with him but he was considerably shaken by the time he reached the safety of the main streets again.

As he collected his baggage from the tavern, one of the maids ceased her polishing to ask, 'Did the lady catch up with you, sir?'

He shook his head, having had put into words what his mind refused to recognize. There was only one person who had known his destination.

Imogen Crowe.

Chapter Sixteen

Faro remembered little of the journey back to Edinburgh, except that the sun was shining as the train steamed into Waverley Station. As he walked along the platform, it was as if the sudden warmth turned all that had happened in Stirling into the interlude from an unpleasant dream.

If only it were so, he thought, as he opened his front door to the welcoming smell of cooking drifting upwards from Mrs Brook's domain. And as he climbed the stairs to his study, cooking was intermingled with beeswax polish.

Mrs Brook had been busy, taking advantage of his absence. The furniture glistened, the windows gleamed. And then he regarded the huge table that also served as his desk.

The chaos that only he understood had been transformed into unrecognizable neat piles of documents. With a gasp of dismay he shrank from this scene of outrage.

Mrs Brook had tidied his papers and books, ignored his stern instructions that they were never to be moved. Angrily, he ran down to the kitchen to confront the housekeeper who was rolling pastry while the maid May peeled apples into a bowl.

Mrs Brook looked up. 'Were you wanting Constable Thomas, sir? He left just a moment ago.'

Her smile of welcome faded before his expression.

'My — my study, Mrs Brook. What the devil do you mean by — disturbing — my desk? You know perfectly well that I'll never be able to find a thing now.'

'I'm sorry, sir, we —' She darted a look at May. 'We were cleaning the upstairs and, while May was polishing, she knocked down some books and papers. It's very easy to do that, sir,' she said quickly in the maid's defence. 'She thought she had better tidy the desk — take the opportunity —'

Faro turned to the maid. 'What the devil do you mean, "take the opportunity", indeed.'

She regarded him fearfully, her mouth slack. As she paused in peeling the apples, he regarded her furiously. Her lips trembled as she shrank back in her chair, cowering away from him.

Even as Mrs Brook stepped forward, murmuring apologies and taking the blame, Faro's anger evaporated into shame that he should rage at a poor servant unable to speak in her own defence.

What on earth was he coming to? He could see the same thought was in Mrs Brook's mind as she regarded him. Her dear gentleman who had never been known to say an unkind word to a servant, or a beggar at the gate. She was shocked, bewildered by his outburst.

Faro sighed, shook his head. 'I shouldn't have shouted at you. Do forgive me. But, please, don't let it happen again, Mrs Brook.'

And to May, with an awkward smile. 'I'm sure

you meant well, lass.' Hoping his tone was conciliatory enough, he returned to his study where two unopened letters awaited his attention.

He recognized Rose's handwriting. Her note contained only a hasty request that Mrs Brook forward her best pair of gloves she had left behind. The second letter, with a London postmark, was from Lachlan. A polite note of thanks with apologies for the delay as his mother had been ill but was recovering. There was no mention of Rose.

Faro sighed with relief. Time was still on his side and he began sorting out his papers, a task that proved less difficult than he had imagined.

It gave him something to concentrate on other than those scenes in Stirling and his homecoming. As he ate a solitary supper, never had he been so conscious of being alone.

He wished Vince were there, like in the old days, when they could sit down together and talk over the day's events.

But Vince had Olivia and they both enjoyed the hectic social life of popular young marrieds.

Sometimes they did little more than exchange greetings at the front door and lately Vince had taken to leaving notes on the hall table to remind him of their plans.

Tonight he was more fortunate. Mrs Brook had just removed his supper tray when Vince put his head round the door.

'You've eaten already, Stepfather. Never mind, you can tell me all about Stirling,' he said, pouring out a glass of wine.

And so Faro related to Vince a somewhat abbreviated version of his meeting with Imogen Crowe and the events that took place in the Stirling Court, omitting the visit to Inchmahome and the near disaster of his walk on the hillside.

'Did you ask her if she ever visited Miss McNair's cottage?' was Vince's first question.

Faro avoided a direct answer, although the description of the young man undoubtedly fitted Seamus Crowe, with flaming red hair and spectacles.

'Of course, what the two ladies saw could have covered a multitude of visitors, all quite coincidental, like the third visitor, a passer-by looking in at the windows mistaking it for a house down the road that was for sale.'

'I doubt that Imogen and her cousin's visit was coincidental considering that we now know there is a Fenian connection,' said Vince.

Faro was silent as he remembered his meeting with John Brown in Lachlan's dressing room at the concert hall. Vince continued, 'The fact that Brown knew the McNairs convinces me that if there is a plot, then he is fully aware of what is at stake.'

Faro sighed. 'I don't doubt you're right, seeing that the Queen is very much under his influence these days.'

'The newspapers and the cartoonists would have us believe she consults him about everything.'

'At least we know the reason why he was so

eager to give the McNairs a decent funeral, burying their secret with them as speedily as possible,' said Faro. 'If only it could be proved —'

'Stepfather,' said Vince severely. 'You can't say you haven't been warned to stay out of it —'

And as Faro made to interrupt, Vince said, 'You haven't the least idea what you're getting into or what these papers contain. You've said so yourself. You're walking in the dark. I know I can't stop you, nor can McIntosh or Brewer —'

'Brewer —' said Faro indignantly.

'They've tried to warn you off, for your own good. As I do now.' And leaning forward he said earnestly, 'I know what you're like, impervious to danger, but do take care, for God's sake, take care.'

'Who is taking care, and what of, pray?' asked Olivia as she bustled into the room, throwing down her bonnet.

'Nothing that you need worry your pretty head about, my dear,' said Vince as she bent down to kiss him. 'How was your meeting this evening?'

'Rather boring. Charitable institutions do attract some not very charitable people into their ranks, I'm afraid.' And to Faro, 'Are you coming to the wedding with us?'

He had forgotten that they were going to Dunblane shortly to Aunt Gilchrist's great-nephew's wedding. Afterwards they planned to go on to Glasgow and visit Rose.

'I haven't received an invitation,' Faro said.

'Dearest Stepfather, you are — family,' Olivia

pointed out gently. 'Besides, everyone's heard of you in Dunblane. Aunt Gilchrist was very proud of being related by marriage to such an important man.'

The thought made Faro groan. He cared little for weddings. Almost as much as he disliked being the centre of attraction and asked absurd questions regarding his police activities.

'It would be such a delight to see Rose, you'd love that,' said Olivia.

It would indeed. But in the days between much was to happen to dispel even that tempting thought from Faro's mind.

Next morning when Faro arrived at the Central Office, Superintendent McIntosh beamed on him. Stirling Constabulary had already been in touch applauding his achievements in the Castle break-in case.

Two days later, returning from the routine of a smuggling crime involving a crew member of the *Erin Star* at Leith, Faro heard the newsboy in Princes Street shouting, 'Irish terrorist commits suicide.'

Chapter Seventeen

Seamus Crowe had hanged himself in his cell in Stirling. The funeral was to be the following day.

And Faro knew he must go. Imogen would be there. She would need someone to turn to who cared about her. Someone who, he hoped, was himself.

At the graveside he saw her, tall, slim, veiled. He was forced to recognize what he already knew, that there was no shadow of doubt that she and her cousin had been the visitors seen by Miss McNair's neighbours. And, sick at heart, he knew why Imogen had been trying to warn him off.

They were Fenians, part of some plot to overthrow the monarchy, a plot hinged on papers stolen from Balmoral Castle. And despite Inspector Brewer's smooth reassurances, their contents had been lethal enough to cost the McNairs their lives.

There were few mourners at the graveside. A sprinkling of prison officials and Imogen. And, hovering at a safe distance, as if he did not care to be recognized, a tall man. Faro frowned. Despite the beard, and a bonnet pulled down well over the man's eyes, Faro was certain they had met before.

'Ashes to ashes, dust to dust —'

As Imogen went forward to throw a handful of

earth on her cousin's coffin, Faro was aware of being watched. Turning, he saw two men, big strong burly men whose faces were partly hidden by their tall hats and upturned collars.

He knew in that instant that these were his attackers on the Mound and the abductors of Bessie McNair. Their presence here declared that it was they, not Imogen, who had fired upon him from the Stirling road. A second attempt on his life that had failed.

Imogen was innocent. And with a surge of triumph he was face to face at last with the murderers of the McNairs.

He sprang into action. They wouldn't get away this time.

Realizing his intention, they turned and went swiftly towards the gate, maintaining dignity until they were out of sight of the group at the graveside. Then they took to their heels.

Faro was lighter, faster on his feet. But they had an escape in readiness; he saw the waiting carriage. The distance between them shortened and he had given no thought to what he would do once he had reached them. Unarmed, it was unlikely that he could overpower them both.

He was unaware of danger. They could hardly turn a rifle on him with so many witnesses. In the forefront of his mind was confrontation, accusation.

It was not to be.

He was within ten yards of his quarry when a shadow leaped out of nowhere, seized him and threw him heavily to the ground.

He struggled, swearing, but the man held him fast, his arms behind his back. Helpless he lay on the ground and, turning his head with difficulty, he looked into the face of the bearded man from the graveside.

'Damn you, let me go. I'm a policeman and those two are escaping.'

The man chuckled and held him fast.

Swearing violently, Faro struggled again. 'You'll pay for this. I'm Inspector Faro of the Edinburgh City Police.'

It was difficult to be convincing or threatening with his face in the gravel and the man laughed again.

'I know full well who you are, sir. Who else could teach me how to hold a man like a trussed chicken?'

And suddenly released Faro found himself looking into the now unfamiliarly bearded face of Detective Sergeant Danny McQuinn.

Faro sprang to his feet. The two men he was pursuing had disappeared. Dusting down his trousers, he glared at McQuinn.

'What do you think you're doing, McQuinn? I'd have caught those two.'

'Precisely, sir. That's what they want. Once inside the carriage —' McQuinn illustrated with a descriptive gesture across his throat.

'But —'

'Come along, sir. We have to talk and it's best we're not seen together.'

With a quick look round McQuinn bundled him into one of the waiting carriages where Faro got a good look at him for the first time. The beard was probably false, dyed hair adding to a ruffianly appearance. Certainly at first glance he was hardly recognizable and Faro would have walked past him in the street.

'What's all this about, McQuinn? I thought you were planning to go to America.'

'Rose told you that, I suppose.' McQuinn laughed. 'I changed my mind. Or had it changed for me.'

'So you're not going after all?' Faro was aware of the disappointment in his voice.

'Not immediately. I have an assignment. I'm back being a loyal Irishman, again. A Fenian in fact —'

'A Fenian?' Faro stared at him in horror.

McQuinn smiled affably. 'That's right, sir, with instructions to infiltrate the movement, find out what's going on over here.'

'You're telling me you're an informer.'

Ignoring Faro's interruption McQuinn continued, 'There's a plot to overthrow the Queen and the government and seeing that I've taken the woman's money, I'm expected to be a decent policeman, loyal, and obedient.'

Pausing he shrugged. 'It's a hard life, sir. I love Ireland and God knows I want to see her freed of English tyranny, but these terrorists are wrong. Bombs and murderers.' He shook his head. 'There has to be some other way.'

151

But Faro wasn't listening and he tried to digest this astonishing information. 'You a police spy, McQuinn. You of all people. It's quite incredible.'

McQuinn ignored that. 'The woman Crowe and her cousin are both in it.'

'Are you sure?' Faro asked, although he knew the answer.

'Certain sure, sir.' As the carriage reached the railway station Faro knew the folly of trying to see Imogen again in the light of this information.

'I presume you're going back to Edinburgh, sir,' said McQuinn consulting his watch. 'We should talk before your train.'

He paid off the coachman and led the way into a dingy, ill-lit public bar across the square. Seated at a squalid beer-soaked table with two pints of ale in front of them, McQuinn asked, 'How much do you know about this latest Fenian activity? I presume that's what has brought you here. You are on to something?' he added eagerly.

'You know as much as me, McQuinn. You were with me when we foiled attempts on the Queen's life,' he added bitterly.

'It's the throne this time. These papers that are missing contain vital information.'

'Exactly what information?' Faro asked.

'Damned if I know. Except that they are of a highly personal and damaging nature.'

'They have to be if the throne is in danger. I presume the Fenians know a bit more than us.'

'Which is what I'm supposed to find out.'

152

'Who are you looking for?'

'A woman.'

'A woman, McQuinn?' Faro laughed.

'Not in the social sense this time,' said McQuinn. 'I only know that the chief member of their spy system over here is a woman who is clever, highly educated, patriotic. Handy with bombs and guns —'

As he spoke Faro had a sinking feeling of disaster and familiarity.

'This is the woman I have to find and eliminate,' McQuinn ended grimly. 'And all I know is that she is in Scotland — somewhere.'

Faro fought back the words and the image that McQuinn had conjured up for him. 'You'll be lucky if you don't end up very dead. How do you know they'll trust you?'

'Because I'm kin to them.'

'A loyal Irish policeman? That's hardly a worthy qualification.'

'I'm a lot more than that. I'm related by blood. You've heard of John O'Mahony?'

Faro nodded. Anyone who had dealings with Ireland had heard of the great patriot and scholar, the historian who had translated a history of Ireland from the Irish.

'It was O'Mahony who chose the name "Fenian" for the new embodiment of Irish national feeling and the word stood for nationhood embodied in the ancient ideal of the *fianna*.' McQuinn paused. 'And O'Mahony was first cousin to my mother.'

'You never told me that,' said Faro accusingly.

'You never asked. I'm using the name O'Mahony by the way, and it's because of my family connection they thought I'd be welcomed with open arms. Fenian is a word for the Irish that is both military and lyrical —'

Faro didn't want another lecture from McQuinn on Irish history. 'I know that. It's been used to describe Irish soldiers for sixty years. I first heard it applied to Irish rebels against the British Empire about ten years ago.'

'It's also used for members of the Irish Republican Brotherhood. It received strong support from our people who suffered in the Famine — and from the harsh treatment of English landlords. As you know, sir, a million and a half people starved to death and another million emigrated. Those who came over here brought death with them, in the form of deadly fevers.'

McQuinn paused. 'My own parents died,' he said sadly. 'And I was brought up in Edinburgh by the Sisters at St Anthony's Orphanage. Others of the family like the O'Mahonys, who survived the coffin ships and reached America, brought a more deadly fever — the passion for revenge.

'The Brotherhood was founded in Dublin on St Patrick's Day in '58 and soon afterwards the Fenians were founded in America, their object to destroy British rule in Ireland. Their sympathies lay with the forced emigrations which gave the Irish Americans a detestation of English rule.

'I know from my folks over there — Rose will

have told you —' He paused and Faro smiled vaguely, amazed that he had known so little about this young man who had shared for several years his daily life with all its danger. 'Rallies of patriotic Fenians ten years ago attracted scores of thousands. Funds were raised by subscriptions, collections and the sale of bonds redeemable when the Irish Republic was established. There was even an issue of postage stamps. I have a few of them, very precious. Armed Fenians paraded in American towns, Fenian newspapers and song books flourished.

'Experienced soldiers from the American Civil War were sent to Ireland to act as instructors and leaders training men for combat. Fenians joined armies as mercenaries, particularly the French Foreign Legion, to gain battle experience. Their activities varied from daring rescues of political prisoners in Ireland, England and Australia to meetings with foreign governments to discuss possible alliances with the offer of Fenian brigades to help any countries fighting Britain. The dearest hope of the Irish Americans was for an Anglo-American war —'

And Faro recalled reading in the *Pall Mall Gazette* in '67 that the Brotherhood was the first case of such a political organization being established in England: 'It will probably annoy us for years and at intervals produce catastrophes . . .'

There was always the fear that a struggle in Ireland might result in American intervention on behalf of Ireland and war with England would develop a sense of national unity between the states.

Faro remembered that the late Charles Dickens had been conscious of the danger and had written: 'If the Americans don't embroil us in a war before long it will not be their fault . . . with their claims for indemnification, what with Ireland and Fenianism and what with Canada, I have strong apprehensions.'

Faro looked through the window at the station clock. 'I must go or I'll miss my train.'

McQuinn nodded. 'Forgive me if I make myself scarce, sir. I can't afford to be seen with a detective in a place as public as a railway station.'

'How do I contact you?'

McQuinn frowned. 'You don't. I can't come to Edinburgh for obvious reasons.'

'What if I have information for you?'

'That's different. There's a jewellery repair shop near the docks in Leith, in Hailes Wynd. There's another just like it, tiny and unobtrusive, here in Wallace Close. If there is no one at home, put a note in the door: "Goods ready. Urgent collection." I'll know it's from you. If the shop is open, which it is on rare occasions, ask for Mr Jacob — that isn't his real name — show him your watch and say, "This was a gift from Mr Lyon, it's gaining time." He'll pass on the message and I'll meet you back there in the public bar.'

'Has Mr Lyon any significance?'

McQuinn laughed. 'Only if you know your Bible, sir. Daniel — my name — in the lion's den, remember?'

As they shook hands, Faro said, 'Take care, McQuinn — I mean O'Mahony.'

McQuinn smiled. 'I will that, sir. You can rely on it. If I'm alive you'll be hearing from me.'

The Edinburgh train had been signalled and as Faro waited on the platform he was aware of being watched.

On the other side of the railway line, he recognized the two men awaiting the train going north as the pair he had pursued in the graveyard.

Without another thought for what the action might cost him, Faro leaped up the stairs and across the line as the Inverness train drew alongside the platform. When the steam subsided a little he realized that the two men had disappeared.

Frantically he ran up and down staring into the windows of the compartments.

'Are you boarding the train, sir?' asked the guard, observing this odd behaviour.

'No. I'm looking for someone.'

'Can't hold the train any longer, I'm afraid.' And so saying he blew his whistle and Faro watched the train slide out of the station.

He heard another whistle and, frantically rushing back over the bridge, was in time to see the Edinburgh train steam away from the platform.

Damn and blast. Damn and blast!

He had lost his quarry and his train. He looked

at the noticeboard and discovered there was a three-hour wait until the next, the last of the day.

He sat on the seat regarding the now empty railway line. And suddenly he didn't care. Maybe destiny was assuming a new role despite McQuinn's revelations. For, having missed his train, the possibility of seeing Imogen again suddenly loomed.

And, at the back of his mind, the teasing thought that she would be in need of some comfort after the day's sadness. The sort of comfort that only a man in love could give a woman.

As he headed back into the town, he decided there was some compensation in disaster after all.

Chapter Eighteen

As he walked out of the railway station Faro realized that he was once again acting on instinct. Taking a chance on Imogen Crowe being alone and spending the night in Stirling, he was drawn back to the same hotel where they had dined the day they went to Inchmahome.

The booking clerk told him that Miss Crowe had Room 16 but her key was not on the board. The man gave him a wry look as he asked for a room near by.

'Room 8, sir.'

As Faro washed his face and regarded his reflection in the mirror, he saw the image of the double bed behind him and reflected upon how this night might end for both of them.

With his hand on the door, he was about to go downstairs to the dining room when a commotion in the corridor alerted him. Running footsteps, raised voices and a woman's scream.

He threw open the door. Imogen Crowe was fighting off an attacker. The gaslit corridor gave too little illumination to identify the man, except that his heavy build suggested to Faro that this was one of the two men he had seen boarding the Inverness train.

At his approach, the man fled and, thrusting Imogen into his room, Faro set off in pursuit, realizing that he had been fooled by an old trick in Stirling railway station. The two men had boarded the train and left it at the signals halt.

As he reached the stairs, he saw that the man had gone. A noisy wedding reception was in progress in the ballroom and he might well have mingled with the crowd.

But Faro's main concern was Imogen. He ran upstairs and found her putting her hair up before the mirror in his room.

'Are you all right?'

She straightened her dishevelled dress. 'Thanks be to God — and that I have a few tricks of self-defence up my sleeve,' and staring ruefully at a torn cuff, she smiled. 'But I've never been so glad to see anyone — when you opened that door. Like an avenging angel, all that was missing was the fiery sword.'

Seeing how pale she was he asked gently, 'What happened? Why were you being attacked?'

She sat down on the bed and stared up at him. For the first time he realized that she was afraid, trembling. 'You know the answer to that, Faro. Better than I do.'

He shook his head. And before he could say a word, she went on, 'Those two men —'

'Men — I only saw one.'

Again she smiled. 'There were two of them. I disabled one on the stairs, left him gasping for breath.'

'Well done, well done,' he whispered.

'His companion recovered quickly enough to

follow me. My room is just along the corridor. But how miraculous to find you here.'

'I missed my train —'

'That's a miracle too. I saw you at the funeral. I hoped to speak to you, but when I turned round you had disappeared. Of course, I understand the reasons why you might not want to be seen in public with a known Fenian.'

'That's not the reason at all, Imogen. The fact was I was chasing your same two men, who I have every reason to believe attacked me in Edinburgh and here in Stirling —'

'You too, Faro? I thought they were on your side.'

He shrugged, not quite ready to bring up the delicate subject of the McNairs and her association with them. 'They are probably hired bullies.'

'They were trying to murder me, right enough, throw me bodily over the stairhead.' She shivered. 'There's a marble floor below. I couldn't possibly have survived. But they'd make it look like an accident — or another suicide.' She turned to him, her eyes full of tears.

'Seamus was murdered, you know. He never hanged himself in his cell. You couldn't get me to believe that. I saw him the night before and he was talking of going back to Ireland to his wife and baby son. Sir Hamish had promised he'd try to get his sentence shortened, perhaps a reprieve if he'd give up what he called terrorist activities, and go home.' She shook her head. 'A good man, Sir Hamish, for a Member of your Parliament.'

Faro did not bother to contradict her and she regarded him thoughtfully. 'You haven't told me why you were chasing those two men, Inspector. Tell me, I'm curious. I thought you were both on the same side,' she repeated, 'fighting Fenians. Why on earth did they attack you in Edinburgh?'

'Because I'm trying to save another damsel in distress.'

'Is that so?' She laughed, as if this were a novel idea.

'Oh yes, I do it all the time. You'd be surprised.'

'And are you always successful?'

'No. Not always,' he replied.

She waited for him to explain further and then went back to smoothing her hair. 'I'm surprised you haven't managed to get yourself a wife then, out of the proceeds. Was your damsel in distress young and beautiful?'

'Quite the contrary. She was poor and plain and middle-aged. I think you were possibly acquainted with her. Her name was Bessie McNair.'

Imogen's brow darkened. There was a moment's confusion. As her eyes slid away from him, declaring her guilt, he knew that she was going to deny all knowledge of the dead woman.

'What makes you think that, Inspector?' she asked softly.

'Because you — and Seamus — were described to me by the sisters who lived next door. They'd seen you at the house.'

She sighed. 'Well, you might as well know the truth, seeing that you know so much already. I

162

was needing background for one of my books and, when I was travelling in Deeside, I stayed at Bessie McNair's cottage. She was a sewing maid to the Queen, you know. So when I was in the Edinburgh area, I decided to look her up again, and take Seamus along.'

Faro shook his head. 'It won't work, Imogen.'

'I don't know what you mean, "it won't work". It's the God's honest truth.'

'According to the two ladies next door, you were there on separate occasions.'

She laughed bitterly. 'Oh that!' Then, with a sigh of resignation, 'You know everything, don't you?'

'I just wondered why a young newspaperman should find her so fascinating. They don't usually waste their time visiting elderly ladies, unless there is a story somewhere.'

'She had been a Royal servant.'

'Why should that be of such great interest to a Fenian?' Again he paused. 'Unless she had something of great value concerning Royalty to hand over to him.' And when she didn't reply, 'Such as stolen secret state papers pilfered from Balmoral.'

She laughed. 'State papers. Is that what they are telling you, Inspector? Well, well.'

'I know they were important enough for your friend Bessie McNair and her brother Davy to be murdered.'

She sat bolt upright, her eyes wide with horror. 'They murdered them. I can't believe it.' She put

163

her hand to her mouth. 'Mother of God, how horrible. And all for a journal and a few letters.'

'What kind of letters?' he demanded sharply.

'Love letters, Inspector.'

'*Love* letters!' Faro exploded.

'Oh yes, and a few drawings and poems. All very personal, letters exchanged between Royal lovers.'

'Who —'

'The Queen, of course. And her trusted servant, John Brown. Mostly from her. She's a great writer of letters, keeps a diary and journal. There's a secret one she carries round with her. If that ever found its way into the wrong hands — There are drawings and poems and she refers to Brown as her husband, moans that she cannot acknowledge him in public. There are some very intimate details — I gather.'

It was Faro's turn to sit back as he remembered a previous occasion when the Queen in love was wildly indiscreet. Except that the object of her abandoned passion was her husband, Prince Albert. Widowed, she had to be restrained by General Sir Charles Grey, her Secretary, from publishing their correspondence with each other, 'including intimate and personal details relating to Her Majesty's marriage which might seem unusual to include in a work intended for general readership'.

If these present documents contained the same passionate and explicit references to lovemaking with John Brown, or were confirmation of a secret

164

marriage made public, they would be dynamite enough to bring down the Royal throne. The scandal would rock the country, the moral old lady who set such high standards for the meanest of her subjects, whoring and drinking with her ghillie.

'Perhaps you can understand why the Fenians want it. They feel that with this as blackmail they might get what they want. Home Rule for Ireland.'

'It's preposterous,' said Faro. 'I've never heard anything so evil — so wicked.'

'On our side — or hers?' said Imogen wryly.

'The ravings of a lovesick, romantic, silly woman have cost three people their lives. Three we know about, the McNairs —' She winced as he continued, 'And your cousin. God only knows how many more have perished, or are in danger.'

'There was another Queen in your Scottish history, I recall, who was foolish and lovesick and her letters destroyed her and cost her love Lord Bothwell his life and sanity,' said Imogen.

History was indeed repeating itself. Faro did not need to be reminded of the 'Casket Letters' which Lord Bothwell, who was not famed for his sentimentality, had rashly kept with him when he was captured in his flight after the Battle of Carberry Hill. Love letters undoubtedly forged but with enough truth in them for Mary Queen of Scots to lose her throne and her head, he thought as Imogen continued.

'Only a few people close to your Queen know

about this journal, which she carries on her person at all times. Her gowns have a secret placket made for it. A small leather book with love sonnets of her own composition which she delighted in reading to John in their private moments.

'While they were at Glen Muick the Queen fell getting out of her carriage. Her voluminous riding dress was torn and muddied and the lady-in-waiting, knowing that Bessie was visiting one of the servants there, took it to her for mending.

'Bessie found the journal. She and Davy weren't great readers, but they realized this was something that might be of considerable value. In fact, it was like manna from heaven for Davy. He'd been under a cloud with the stablemen and the locals, gambling, and losing heavily. He was under notice to leave the Castle. Bessie was distraught. Apparently, she had been trying to help him pay off his debts by carrying off the odd piece of china, a silver spoon or two from the Castle — nothing that would be missed or recognized — and selling them in Ballater.

'Now, with the journal in their possession, they felt their troubles were over. They left straightaway, while the going was good, especially as the Queen was still a little confused, having hit her head when she fell. It wasn't until she got back to Balmoral that she discovered the journal had gone and all hell broke loose. She thought she had lost it on the fatal ride; it wasn't until much later she learned the truth. John Brown guessed that Bessie McNair had stolen it.'

'But how did it get into Fenian hands?'

Imogen bit her lip. 'It hasn't — yet. Oh, the McNairs hadn't any preference for Fenians in particular. All they wanted was someone who would pay them good money. I don't imagine they guessed the power they had in their hands at that moment, the contents of a journal that could be used to bring down the monarchy. You see, all they recognized was the Queen's signature, or Brown's, and the occasional name and words of endearment, but the ambiguities, the love language and *double entendres* were quite beyond them.

'They needed someone to tell them what it was worth. And Bessie remembered that I was a writer and I had given her a forwarding address, because some of the people I had met might have notes to send on for my book. When I heard from her that she had a journal that belonged to the Queen, I wasn't particularly interested but guessed that it was Seamus's territory. I gave her his address.'

She paused. 'You know the rest. Almost. Seamus got in touch with her in Edinburgh by this time. She was fly enough not to let him see the whole journal but gave him a couple of pages, just to let him see it was authentic. It was enough for him to guess that this was explosive material, far more effective for his Fenian comrades than a dozen bombs or ineffectual assassination attempts.

'But however fast he moved, the Queen was faster. It hadn't taken long for them to guess that the journal was with the McNairs. Time was of the essence and by the time we visited the cottage, at Bessie's request, she had gone.'

She stopped and sighed. 'We couldn't understand it. Now I do. The poor woman was already dead, murdered as you say. Seamus went in search of Davy and when he didn't find him, his fellow comrades were very upset. They still are. They desperately want to lay their hands on this journal.'

'Who is their contact over here?' When she didn't reply, he added sharply, 'It is you?'

She laughed. 'Sure now, you can't expect me to answer that honestly. A loyal Irishwoman like myself giving away such vital information to a policeman.' She paused and added bitterly, 'A woman with good reason to hate the English who murdered her uncle and her cousin and who has served time at Her Majesty's pleasure in one of her hellish prisons. Surely you can understand that.'

'Yes, I understand even if I think you're wrong. But I'm not involved in the Fenian part of it unless they also happen to be the McNairs' killers.'

Imogen shook her head. 'They weren't Fenians, I can assure you of that,' she said. 'They were murdered by your own people, the same that murdered Seamus.'

'Not my people, Imogen, not the police. We're here to establish law and order, not to murder people. Our law is justice for the guilty and freedom for the innocent.'

'You tell me that?' she laughed. 'I've tasted your justice. And I'm as keen as anyone to see justice for Bessie and Davy McNair. And to see their murderers hanged. But there isn't a snow-flake in hell's chance of that. Your assassins are in the direct employ of your government, sanctioned by the Queen herself.'

Faro realized that Imogen was right. There was nothing he could say.

'Seeing that you're not involved, Inspector, I'll tell you something that might surprise you. Your own ranks are not without Fenian supporters. There are even Irish policemen who are on our side.'

Faro pretended surprise. 'You can't make me believe that,' he lied, thinking about McQuinn.

Imogen stood up. 'I had better go now.'

'Where are you going?'

'Back to my room, of course.'

Faro shook his head. 'No, you're not. You're going to stay here tonight —'

'But —'

'You are going to sleep in that bed and I'll sleep on the sofa where I can keep watch.'

He could see she was glad to have him there. 'Not a very amicable arrangement,' she said softly.

He pretended not to hear her. He was already in so deep that it could destroy him. What she had told him had confirmed his growing suspicion that McQuinn was right and Imogen Crowe was more than she pretended to be.

Somehow he had to get the information to McQuinn regarding the contents of those so-called state documents, information that everyone who encountered them was so eager to keep secret. And for very good reason. Never before had the throne been in such danger. If they were made public, the monarchy, unsteady as it was, would topple.

At least it kept his mind away from the slight figure who was sleeping so peacefully in the bed just yards away. And from thoughts of how this night might have ended.

He had been in love before, wanted a woman as much as he wanted Imogen Crowe, but to start a relationship with a woman who was also the Fenians' agent in Scotland was a sufficient dampener on his ardour.

He did not sleep much that night.

Chapter Nineteen

Soon after daybreak, Faro fell into a fitful dream-laden sleep broken by the sounds of a busy hotel's awakening.

Turning his head, his neck stiff and sore, every bone aching with the discomfort of the hard sofa, he saw that Imogen's bed was empty.

Perhaps she had returned to her own room. Putting on his jacket, he hurried down the hall. But Room 16 was empty, a maid already changing sheets on the bed.

Downstairs the desk clerk yawned sleepily, told him Miss Crowe had left very early.

'Paid her bill' — and pausing to consult the ledger — 'left no forwarding address, sir,' he added, with an impudent look as if he had already put his own interpretation on the nocturnal activities between Rooms 8 and 16 that night.

In no mood for breakfast, Faro left the hotel and wandered around the almost empty streets hoping that he might meet her. At last he gave up.

He should contact Danny McQuinn with his new information. Not wishing to draw attention to his interest in Wallace Close by asking directions, he found it at last with considerable difficulty and an inadequate map.

Twice he wandered past the window marked

'Jewellery Repairs' in faded paint. McQuinn could hardly have chosen a less prepossessing contact. The door was locked, the window barred and padlocked. The Close had a look of long desertion, foul-smelling, a resting place for stray cats and the debris abandoned by undesirable worthies of the human variety furthered its seedy appearance.

It didn't look as if Mr Jacob did much business and Faro put a note in the door with little hope that McQuinn would ever see it.

'Goods ready. Please collect. F.'

Eager to breathe fresh air again, he hurried towards the station and waited for half an hour on the chilly platform, a very frustrated man. There were many questions he should have asked McQuinn when he had the chance. In particular his intentions regarding Rose.

When the train arrived, he looked out of the window on a landscape cold and grey as his own heart, with the colours drained away as they had from his own life.

Where was Imogen now? He loved her, wanted her desperately. He longed to wake up every morning for the rest of his life and find her dear head on the pillow beside him. He wanted her for his wife but, even as he recognized the depths and longing of his desire, he knew it could never come true.

Imogen had known it too. When they met in Elrigg, both had become beguiled by the chemistry of physical and mental attraction. But that was no guarantee of a lifetime's devotion. Beyond passion lurked the just causes and impediments, a policeman and a writer who belonged to that new race of independent womanhood, free from the bondage of husband and family, free to move where and when she chose.

Faro had little to offer in return. Only the uncertainties of his own life, a vast chasm ever deepening between them. He knew that one day he would not be quite quick enough, his deductions not quite sharp enough and he would meet death at the hands of a quicker, younger opponent.

These uncertainties had always existed, even in his marriage to Vince's mother, Lizzie. Now they had intensified with the passing years and he had even less security to offer as a husband.

What was he thinking about? A Chief Inspector of Police bound in marriage to a known Irish Fenian?

He sat up with a jerk.

'This is the terminus, sir.' The guard tapped on the compartment window and grinned. 'As far as we go.'

Through the steam he saw the platform of Waverley Station, the Castle grim against the skyline, the gardens shrouded, unwelcoming as he walked home towards Newington, sharing his unhappy thoughts with the bleak greyness around him.

Mrs Brook met him at the door. 'You've just missed Charlie — I mean, Constable Thomas, sir. He had a message for you.'

'What was it, Mrs Brook?'

She shook her head. 'He said it was important and he would leave it at the Central Office.'

There was no message from Thomas, but the constable at the desk said, 'He rushed out in a great hurry. Said he was going to Leith.'

The word Leith conjured up McQuinn's contact. Constable Thomas was sharp and efficient. Had he stumbled on something vital concerning the secret organization?

In the hope that he might meet the constable *en route*, Faro headed towards Hailes Wynd, a dingy-looking close adjacent to Weighman's Close on the opposite side of the road to Mrs Carling's establishment.

There was no sign of Thomas and Faro walked with caution into the dim and solitary depths of the narrow alleyway where he had some difficulty locating the jewellery repair shop. If that were possible, it looked even more decrepit than its counterpart in Stirling.

Faro stared through the barred window at a few tired-looking dust-covered watches, clocks and trinkets long since forsaken by their owners.

The jeweller was clearly not at home and Faro slipped under the door the message for McQuinn with even less hope that it would ever reach him.

Back at his desk, with a refreshing lack of homicides and sudden death, he faced the sordid and tedious routine of robberies with violence and

174

lesser crimes. He was sorting through the documents left for him, trying to find what was most interesting, when Superintendent McIntosh looked around the door.

'Wondered what happened to you, Faro. Heard you'd gone back to Stirling in connection with this Irish terrorist who committed suicide.'

'That is so, sir. Anything to do with Fenians is something we must keep to the forefront of our minds,' said Faro, looking appropriately stern.

'And what did you find?'

'Nothing vital, sir, that need concern us.'

McIntosh stared at him suspiciously, aware somehow that he was not being told the whole truth. Then with a shrug he murmured, 'Fenians, eh? Good fellow. Keep at it,' and withdrew.

Faro wondered how his superior would have reacted to the information that Detective Sergeant McQuinn late of the Edinburgh City Police, was now part of a counter-spy service. Edinburgh and Stirling were no doubt only two of the links in the chain, but the fact that such an organization existed without the knowledge of Superintendent McIntosh, who imagined that he knew everything and was in everyone's confidence, would fill that gentleman with a sense of outrage.

Returning to his documents with a weary sigh, Faro was interrupted by a knock on the door. This time it was Constable Lamont, Thomas's partner on the Newington beat.

'I'm looking for Charlie — Constable Thomas that is, sir.'

'Why should you expect to see him here?'

'He had an urgent message for you.'

'So I understand.'

Lamont nodded. 'Wouldn't trust it to anyone, not even myself, sir, and that's unusual for Charlie. Tells me everything generally. All he'd say was in strictest confidence, that this is something the chief should know about. Quite excited, he was. Never seen him so pleased and he insisted that he had something to tell you. I gathered it was a message or suchlike he wanted to deliver personally. "I just want to see his face." Those were his very words, sir.'

Lamont looked anxious and Faro said, 'He came to the house today while I was absent. I didn't attach a great deal of importance to his visit.' He smiled and added, 'I gather he did that quite a lot.'

Lamont grinned. 'He's very seriously courting, sir, as you probably know. Looks like Mrs Brook will be losing her little maid.' The constable shook his head. 'But this was really urgent, sir. As I said, he was in quite a state. "This is what the chief's looking for. And I think I've cracked the case for him. You'll hear about it in due course. But I have to know for sure first." And without another word, he was off again.'

Lamont shook his head. 'I haven't seen him since. That was two days ago. I don't want to report it, sir, as you know I'm supposed to, when the constable I share the beat with fails to turn up for duty.'

He looked at Faro. 'What shall I do, sir? I don't want to get him into trouble.'

Faro frowned. Thomas was ambitious, clever. The last constable not to turn up for duty without a very good reason. He came to a sudden decision.

'Report it, Lamont. Say that P.C. Thomas is on special duty concerning an inquiry for Chief Inspector Faro. Get them to give you a temporary replacement. I'll take full responsibility.'

But the constable's absence disturbed him. The only case Thomas and he had been involved in that 'could be cracked' remained the McNair murders.

When he returned home that evening, he found Mrs Brook alone in the kitchen. Asked if Constable Thomas had called, she shook her head.

'No, indeed, sir. Haven't seen hair nor hide of him since he left the message for you.' Suddenly she stood up straight and said, 'I might as well tell you, sir, that I'm not at all pleased the way things are going. That young man is never out of my kitchen, not that I object to him personally, he's nice enough in his way, but he keeps distracting May who isn't the most efficient of maids, you will gather. I don't feel that my kitchen is my own, any more, with the two of them cuddling and kissing whenever my back is turned. Frankly, sir, I'll be glad when they get married.'

Faro's eyes widened. This was the longest

speech he had ever heard Mrs Brook make and obviously one she had been considering for some time.

He smiled. 'You've always had a great ordeal putting up with us and we are most grateful, especially with our uncertain hours, and your excellent cooking so often ruined.'

But Mrs Brook wasn't yet finished.

'I know that, sir, but I never minded. You were my two very special gentlemen — and I could rely on you in so many ways.' She shook her head. 'This isn't like what it was in the old days, the household running smooth as silk, upstairs and downstairs too. I've always managed fine on my own.'

She sighed. 'Young maids are nothing but trouble, sir, if you ask me. I was always told they were the bane of a housekeeper's life and now I know that for the truth.'

And, having completed her speech, Mrs Brook turned towards the oven, looked inside and said, 'You'll be wanting your supper, sir. I'll bring it up to your study directly, Dr Vince and Mrs Laurie had theirs before leaving for the theatre.'

Faro went upstairs. His fears were being realized that two separate households were needed and that it had been a mistake to let Olivia and Vince persuade him to stay in Sheridan Place after their marriage.

Life would be further complicated for poor Mrs Brook when the new baby arrived. There would have to be a nanny and a housemaid to do the extra washing. He could not see the housekeeper coping with that kind of disorganization in her domain.

But the problems of domesticity were temporarily dismissed as he opened the daily *Scotsman* where his attention was immediately drawn to a paragraph headed: 'Success for Famous Scottish Pianist'. Lachlan Brown's First Piano Concerto had been given its début in London . . . Royalty had been present . . . It ended, 'Anyone fortunate enough to hear this tremendous work could be left in no doubt of Mr Brown's future as a composer.'

Faro's thoughts as to how this success might also influence his daughter's future relationship with Lachlan were dismissed by the insistent ringing of the front doorbell.

Voices were raised in the hall and he ran downstairs to see the police carriage outside his door.

Constable Lamont leaped out and rushed up the steps.

'It's Charlie Thomas, sir. He's in Leith. Been stabbed. He's asking for you. Come quickly, sir. He's dying.'

Chapter Twenty

As the police carriage raced towards the scene of Constable Thomas's attack, Faro felt numbed by this totally unexpected development.

Casualties among policemen were not unusual, there were hazards in plenty, his own father had been a victim. Many had died in accidents and fights during his thirty years' service with the City Police. Some were young men at the beginning of promising careers but few he had encountered were like Thomas, born policemen. Thomas, Faro was certain, by dint of hard work and high intelligence would have risen very soon to the rank of sergeant-detective and ultimately to that of inspector.

And now his short life was at an end. He knelt by his side and took hold of his cold hands.

'Such a waste, such a terrible waste,' he said, his eyes filled with tears.

The elderly constable who had discovered Thomas cleared his throat and said, 'He died just minutes ago, sir. He asked for you, trying to ask you something or other.' He sighed heavily. 'He was a good man, sir, he didn't deserve this.'

As they put Thomas into the carriage, Faro was aware of Lamont sobbing, wiping his eyes with a large handkerchief.

'He was my friend, sir. My friend,' he said. 'I'll

kill the bastard who did this — if it's the very last thing I do.'

'We'll find him, Lamont, we'll find him.'

Trying to calm the young constable helped Faro deal with his own grief. He was aware that the stabbing had taken place just yards away from the boarding house, where they had gone together to interview Mrs Carling who now gazed cautiously over a neighbour's shoulder. Her son Andy was nowhere in evidence.

This wasn't Thomas's beat. He had no right to be in this area unless he was on official business. Staring hard in the woman's direction, he wondered did that business concern the Carlings and their possible connection with the McNair murders?

('I think I've cracked the case for the chief.')

Thomas's excitement and Lamont's reported words came back to him. Messages left at Sheridan Place and the Central Office could only concern the McNairs, the case they had worked on together and the only reason for Thomas being so far away from Newington.

Faro would no doubt find out once the constable's killer was caught. Meanwhile there were the practical matters concerning sudden death to be dealt with.

'Had he any family?' he asked Lamont.

'Yes, sir. His mother lives in Crail.' Lamont's surprised look indicated that he expected Faro to know that.

Faro was guiltily aware how little he knew of

Constable Thomas. He had just learned that his first name was Charlie. For all the young man's reliability and worth, Faro realized that he had never made the effort to know him better. He had no curiosity regarding his private life beyond an amused tolerance that the constable was courting the maid in his own household.

This situation was by no means unique. It had characterized his entire association with Danny McQuinn, despite years of working together. On more than one occasion McQuinn's prompt action had saved Faro's life, but all he knew of him was that he came from Ireland and had been brought up in the Catholic orphanage of an Edinburgh convent.

Rose had added information regarding McQuinn's relatives in the United States but not until their unexpected meeting in Stirling had he learned the significant facts of McQuinn's upbringing.

Faro considered this deficiency in the character of a man whose whole life was involved in tracking down clues. A man who saw himself as one who cared deeply for his fellow men and would fight any injustice on their behalf. Did this grave omission exist in his personality alone or were all senior officers so afflicted with indifference, regarding their policemen as little more than soulless drones to drive carriages, carry messages, smooth out the dull and exhaustive patches of criminal investigations.

And it struck Faro as despicable to learn only

after the young man was dead that he had a private life.

He turned to Lamont. 'I had better inform Mrs Thomas.'

'No need for that, sir, unless you particularly wish to do so.' There was an embarrassed silence. 'You see, sir, I've visited her with Charlie several times.' He paused. 'It'll come easier from me, sir, seeing I was his friend.'

'Thank you, Lamont. I appreciate your action. I will of course send an official letter, and so will Superintendent McIntosh.'

As he said the words, Faro was aware of his own hypocrisy, of being overwhelmed with feelings of relief that he had been spared the ordeal of breaking tragic news to a bereaved parent. He was also guiltily aware that he had been secretly hoping Lamont would make the offer.

There was a little pause, then Lamont cleared his throat and said, 'Someone will need to tell his sweetheart, sir. It'll break the poor lass's heart. They were hoping to wed, you know.'

'I'll tell her, Lamont,' said Faro, wondering how on earth he would convey such dire news to a girl who could not even speak.

At the Central Office, a full investigation into Thomas's death was set in motion. Witnesses in the area would be questioned, policemen alerted for information regarding suspicious persons and guilty behaviour.

Thomas had been struck in a main artery, his

killer could not have escaped without his clothing being considerably stained with blood.

It was late afternoon before Faro returned home, anticipating the dreaded interview with May.

His arrival coincided with Mrs Brook bustling along the road with her basket of groceries. 'Quite a stir we had, sir, getting them away.'

Faro stared at her. Getting who away? The events of the early morning and his speedy departure had swept from his mind that Vince and Olivia were leaving for the wedding at Dunblane.

'You'll be needing something to eat, sir —'

'No, not now, Mrs Brook, thank you.'

'A nice cup of tea, then?'

He felt in dire need of something much stronger than tea but followed her downstairs, rehearsing the words he was going to say to break the news to the maid. He was greatly relieved to find her absent, doubtless out on some errand for Mrs Brook.

His wan appearance hadn't escaped the housekeeper's vigilance. She was curious about the Inspector's appearance in her kitchen since he usually went straight up to his study.

'Is there something I can get you, sir?'

When he shook his head, she said, 'If you'll go upstairs, I'll bring you a tray directly.'

Faro sat down heavily at the table. 'Mrs Brook, I have some bad news —'

She turned to him anxiously, her hands holding the teapot trembled. 'Oh, sir, what is it? Oh dear — not one of the family?'

'No, Mrs Brook. Not the family. Now, please do sit down.' And when she did so, he said, 'It's Constable Thomas, he's been stabbed in a fight.'

'Oh, poor Charlie.' She looked at him. 'May will be worried about him. He's not seriously hurt, is he?'

'I'm afraid so. He died earlier this morning.'

Mrs Brook gave a little scream and covered her face with her hands. 'Oh, not that nice young man.' She regarded him tearfully. 'How we are going to break this to May when she gets back, I don't know.'

'Will she be long?'

'Long, sir? Why, she's away to Dunblane with Dr Vince and Mrs Laurie. Rushes in at the last minute, hands me a note that the young mistress wants her with them.' Pausing she shook her head. 'I don't know what this house is coming to, really I don't. All these notes. And now poor Charlie killed. He was sitting just where you are —'

She put a hand to her mouth. 'I've just remembered something. Oh dear —' She went over to the sideboard and took a large envelope out of a drawer. 'This was for May. Charlie left it for her. How do I give this to her now? It'll break the poor lass's heart.'

She placed the envelope on the table. 'It's for her birthday. That's tomorrow. I should have remembered and given it to her before she left.

But with all the confusion, it went clean out of my mind.'

Pausing, she looked across at Faro. 'Charlie wanted it to be a surprise. Poems he'd written, that sort of thing. A bit of nonsense I thought for, bless the poor dear lad's heart, he's the romantic one — she's the practical kind. While he was explaining that he wanted it to be waiting for her at her bedside when she woke up, she came in, back from the shops. So he tipped me a wink and said sternly, "This is for Inspector Faro, Mrs Brook. Very important. You see that he gets it. Put it on his desk right away. Understand?" And off they went together.' She sighed. 'What'll I do now, sir?'

Faro shook his head. 'Explain it all to her when she comes back. Maybe she'll understand and it will be something for her to remember him by.'

On the following day, Thomas's killer was apprehended.

Constable Bevan, on duty at Waverley Station and, on the lookout for a sneak thief operating on the railway, had noticed a man in a great hurry, his clothes covered in bloodstains, heading towards the platform where the London train was about to depart.

He had no ticket and when the guard refused to let him through the barrier, he hurled the unfortunate man to the ground and, running along the platform, flung open a compartment door and jumped aboard as the train gathered speed.

Constable Bevan ran to the Telegraph Office and alerted stations along the line. The man's bloodied appearance, his suspicious behaviour, had been observed by a frightened passenger who pulled the communication cord. He thereupon leaped from the compartment and tumbled down the steep embankment.

By the time the policemen reached him, he was unconscious, badly injured and unlikely to live.

They took him to the City Hospital where the contents of his coat revealed Thomas's pocket watch identified by Lamont. Also a purse containing twenty sovereigns. The man, Jack Byrne, was well known to the officers.

The surrounding policemen eyed it grimly. Such a sum of money was practically a confession that he had been paid to kill the constable.

And by a person or body of persons who had plenty of money and were very anxious that Thomas and his precious information should go no further, thought Faro as he elected to sit by Byrne's bedside in the hope that he might survive long enough to reveal the present whereabouts of the constable's official notebook. Its absence from his possessions suggested that it might hold vital clues to his murderer's employers.

As he took up his vigil Faro regarded Byrne's brutal countenance with distaste and despair. It was of little comfort to know that a 'wanted for murder' notice had long been posted for this habitual criminal who lived in the thieves' kitchen at Causewayside. He had been in and out of gaol

187

since his youth, having known nothing as refined as schooldays, a paid killer, a man who would maim for a shilling and kill for a couple of sovereigns.

And this was Thomas's killer. Thomas had apparently tried to arrest him in Leith. If Byrne lived, he would go to the gallows, denied the claim of self-defence, that the constable had charged him in connection with a crime he knew nothing about. Resisting arrest, Byrne had fought him off, drawing the knife he always carried as a deterrent whereupon Thomas had somehow fallen on it.

Byrne never had the chance to put it all into words this time. Sometime during Faro's vigil, he opened his eyes and asked for water. Holding the glass to his lips, Faro asked, 'Who paid you to kill the policeman?'

Byrne shook his head. 'Don't know — nothing.'

'What do you know of the McNairs?'

'The McNairs.' The man shook his head. He closed his eyes with a heavy sigh and any hopes of further information were over for good. Blood bubbled through his lips and Jack Byrne was dead. He had escaped the hangman's rope.

But the questions remained unanswered. It had been presumed that Thomas was trying to arrest him, but Faro guessed that most likely Thomas had been lured to Weighman's Close on some pretext of information and that Byrne had been waiting ready to knife him.

Faro remembered seeing Mrs Carling as he

188

knelt by Thomas. He was certain there was a connection with the McNairs and that it centred on Mrs Carling and her son Andy.

'I think I've cracked the case for the chief.'

His words continued to haunt Faro as he set off to interview the Carlings.

He was unlucky. The door was locked.

'Away for the day,' was the laconic answer from a neighbour with as little desire as Mrs Carling for any dealings with the police, especially when one of their colleagues had been killed in the vicinity. The woman and the other members of her household had already been closely questioned as possible witnesses.

'Tell her I'll be back,' said Faro.

Chapter Twenty-One

The coolness of Faro's reception by Mrs Carling when he arrived at the close next day confirmed his suspicions that she and her son probably knew a great deal more about Constable Thomas's death and the events preceding it than they were prepared to admit.

He was not unexpected. The neighbours must have warned her.

'Is your son at home?'

'No, he isn't.'

'When are you expecting him?'

'I don't know. He's away — to Glasgow — looking for work,' she added defensively. 'A good lad, keen to get on, you know.'

Faro regarded her sternly. 'You are aware that the constable who was with me last time was stabbed almost outside your door.'

She winced. 'Everyone in the close knew about it.'

'And yet no one went to his assistance.'

Her laugh was shrill and unhappy and she looked at him as if he had taken leave of his senses to entertain such an idea. As with the rat-infested closes off the High Street, he guessed that at the first sign of trouble people swiftly withdrew into their own houses and closed the doors firmly until it was passed.

Anyone accused of cowardice asked simply: What was to be gained by getting a knife stuck in you? or: We all have troubles enough of our own, mister, without going out looking for other folk's.

Mrs Carling, however, recovered her composure enough to say, 'A terrible thing to happen outside a respectable boarding house. How this will affect my gentlemen, I don't know. They'll be afraid to sleep in their beds. And my livelihood will suffer. I'll be in the workhouse in no time,' she added wringing her hands convincingly.

'Did you see Constable Thomas that day? Had he called at your house recently?'

Her eyes wavered uncertainly. 'He was around the close quite a lot lately. Very unnerving it was, a uniformed policeman sniffing about, as if we were guilty of some crime. Gives a respectable house a bad name.'

As she spoke Faro suddenly sprang across to the door. He moved so lightly and soundlessly that when he flung it open, Andy Carling catapulted into the room, his mother's warning scream a second too late.

'Back from Glasgow already,' said Faro amiably. 'No need to listen at keyholes, lad.'

'I wasn't — just came in. Heard Ma had a visitor. I was curious.'

'So we see. Well, now that you're here make yourself at home,' said Faro leading him to the table and pushing him into a chair. Sitting opposite, he said, 'Now what have you to tell me about

191

Constable Thomas's visits?'

Andy exchanged an uneasy glance with his mother. 'It had nothing to do with us.'

'So you know what I'm on about,' said Faro. 'That's a relief. We're looking for reliable witnesses to the incident.'

'I don't know anything about him being stabbed. The man what did it, everyone knows he's a killer and keeps wide of him. They got into an argument, that's all we know.'

Mrs Carling put her hand on her son's arm. 'Will he need to go to the court?' she asked anxiously, her mind clearly dealing with many other crimes that might be unmasked.

'I don't think that will be necessary, seeing that the constable's killer is dead. Jumped from a moving train.'

'Well, well,' said Mrs Carling in tones of obvious relief. 'At least my laddie is saved the ordeal. This sort of thing is so bad for a lad's reputation.'

Faro smiled grimly. And young Andy's shady activities were safe from exposure for a little longer.

'You'd better tell the Inspector what he wants to know.'

'I don't know nothing, Ma. You know that. I'd have told you.' Andy whined.

Faro stood up. There was nothing more he could do, except waste time trying to wrest information out of the Carlings.

'If you change your mind, or if your mother

persuades you to do so, you know where to find me.'

Number 9 Sheridan Place was silent, empty. As Faro wearily climbed the stairs to his study he realized that Vince and Olivia would not return from the wedding in Dunblane until Wednesday.

But on Wednesday, Vince came home alone. He had persuaded Olivia to take a few extra days at the famed Hydro.

'Such indulgences are necessary in the early days of pregnancy, Stepfather. And she had May to look after her. They'll be back with Rose at the weekend. What's been happening to you in our absence?'

Vince listened intently as Faro brought him up to date. He too was shocked by Constable Thomas's death and the reverberations this would have on Olivia's maid, whom, according to Mrs Brook and Constable Lamont, he intended to marry.

'What a dreadful blow for that poor afflicted girl.'

As Faro laid a wreath on Thomas's grave overlooking the sea in Crail, his thoughts were with May.

Vince had sent a telegraph to Olivia, telling her of the constable's death, and Faro expected to see the maid among the female relatives and friends gathered in Thomas's home, since it was not the usual practice in Scotland for women to accompany the coffin to the graveside.

But May was not in evidence. Constable Lamont looked round and shook his head sadly. 'Shouldn't be surprised if she's had a complete collapse with shock, poor lass. 'Sides she's never met Charlie's mother or his family —'

The tearful, sad-eyed group of women clung together in the white-washed fisherman's cottage in a close by the harbour. The constable's father laboured painfully to attend the needs of the mourners, offering drams, receiving their murmured condolences with a shake of his head, a grief-stricken parent walking through a nightmare from which there was no awakening.

All his hopes had been buried with his only son in that grave near the stormy shore where the winds already played havoc with the bright wreaths so reverently laid.

And Faro had brought home to him that day the similarity of his own family history to that of Charlie Thomas. His father was son of a poor Orkney crofter scraping a living from the sea. But Magnus Faro had been clever the 'lad o'parts'. Sacrifices had been made to send him to the Scottish mainland to fulfil his heart's desire and become a policeman.

Magnus had done well, only to be run down by a carriage in Edinburgh's hilly High Street late one night — murdered, as his son was to prove many years later — because his disclosures in the case of the mummified infant in the wall of Edinburgh Castle, perhaps the rightful King

James VI, put the Royal succession in jeopardy.

Faro had been four years old. His mother Mary took him back to Orkney where she in her turn made sacrifices for his education and upbringing, so that he might follow in his late father's footsteps.

She had watched him leave with unspoken forebodings, but her fears that history might repeat itself had been unfounded and Chief Detective Inspector Jeremy Faro was touching the pinnacle of a brilliant career. The next step would be Superintendent, a step he had little desire to take for it meant sitting behind a desk issuing orders.

A safe job, but not one cut out for him, he thought as he boarded the train and sat glumly silent beside Lamont and his colleagues returning to Edinburgh after the young constable's funeral.

Never had he been so thankful to see the welcoming lamps in his own windows. He would be glad to shed the miasma of sorrow, share a drink with Vince and chat over the problems of a successful young doctor's practice.

He heard voices in the drawing room.

Olivia was home.

He threw open the door, called a greeting.

Olivia was holding Vince's hand as they sat alone close together by the fire. Something in their attitudes, in the shocked countenances they turned towards him, had his heart leap in a shaft of terror.

'Rose? Isn't she with you?' Faro demanded.

Olivia shook her head and began to cry.

Chapter Twenty-Two

Faro dashed to Olivia's side. 'Rose — is something wrong with Rose?'

Vince put a hand on his arm. 'I'm sure Rose is all right, she's been delayed, that's all,' he said smoothly. 'However, Olivia — Olivia has something to tell you, Stepfather. You had better sit down.'

So saying, he poured a dram and thrust it into Faro's hand. 'Now, dearest, please tell him what you know.'

Olivia nodded miserably, twisting the lace handkerchief around her fingers. 'At the beginning, it was just a trivial mistake, the kind of incident that happens to us all.'

She paused and sighed. 'You remember the day Rose and I went to Duddingston Fair?'

'I do indeed. That was also the day you announced your delightful news.'

Olivia wavered, her hand went immediately protectively to her stomach. She nodded. 'Rose had promised to look up the great-aunts of one of her favourite pupils. And they were there, two dear old souls, sisters, full of chatter, bright as squirrels —'

Her description brought Bessie McNair's chatty neighbours vividly before Faro.

'They looked at May — I had called her forward to help carry some of the things I had bought at their stall. She seemed reluctant, she always behaved shyly, as you know, but, for a moment, she didn't seem to hear me and she seemed to — shrink away from them.

'I laughed a little at her keeping her head well down as she gathered our purchases together. The sisters were chattering like magpies to another customer, suddenly one of them looked up and said, "Oh, it's you, dear, I thought I recognized you." And the other sister came forward at that. "Did you find the house that was for sale all right?"

'Well, May just stared at them blankly and, with a quick glance at me, hurried away with Rose, clasping her parcels. I was curious. I wanted to know what it was all about. I waited till they had served the next customer and then I said, "You know my maid?"

' "Not exactly," said one, "but we've met before."

' "When was that?" I asked.

'They were more than willing to tell me. "Your maid, is she? She came to look for a house in Duddingston. There was a cottage next door to us, and we saw her peering in the windows. Apparently she was looking for a house. We told her it wasn't for sale." '

Olivia paused, made a helpless gesture, 'I thought, the sly thing keeping it to herself, so I told them we gathered that she was going to marry our local policeman. They looked puzzled

197

at that because she had said the house was too small for her. With a husband and four wee bairns.'

Olivia stopped breathless and looked from Vince to Faro.

'I asked them, "You mean, she actually spoke to you?" They were both emphatic about that and an argument followed about who said what to whom, which I interrupted to ask if they were absolutely sure we were talking about the same person. They said of course they were sure, her accent being Irish, like their dear mother.

'I was shattered at being deceived by her. Pretending not to be able to speak. It took me all my time to be civil to her on the way home, I can tell you.'

She was silent for a moment and Faro remembered their return from the fair and Rose saying that someone had recognized May and wasn't it a small world.

And Faro cursed himself for not listening more carefully, detaching himself as he always did from any domestic chitchat, when he might have learned so much —

Olivia sighed and continued. 'I was fairly shattered at her pretending to be dumb, but I told myself the two ladies might be mistaken and, when I mentioned it to her — tactfully, she just shook her head wildly, indicating that she must have a double.

'I realized that was probably true. She's a plain little thing and the two ladies, well, let's face it, they did seem a bit dotty. Anyway, I determined to forget about it.'

She stopped and took a sip of water.

'When we were in Dunblane for the wedding, Vince decided that after he left May should go to Glasgow and bring Rose back to the Hydro, that we would be company for each other.'

Again, she paused and Vince patted her hands. 'You'd better continue, dearest, if you're up to it. Or shall I tell Stepfather the rest?'

'No. No.' Olivia sat up straight. 'At the wedding reception, I had met an old friend of Aunt Gilchrist who, I discovered, was also staying at the Hydro. At breakfast, in the course of our conversation, the inevitable subject of maids came up.

'She said, "Your poor dear aunt was so shattered when hers died of a fever. She loved that poor dumb creature, treated her like a daughter. We were sure it hastened her end —" I couldn't believe what I was hearing. I asked her to repeat it —'

Olivia paused, shook her head. 'There was no longer the slightest doubt. The maid was May Moray. May, whom she'd taken from the orphanage, who had been with her for six years. The friend went on to say how Aunt had told everyone that when she died her great niece — me — was to take care of her.'

She looked at them both, smiled sadly. 'Aunt Gilchrist had told everyone how proud she was that I had married into such an illustrious household, with a Chief Inspector of Police as stepfather-in-law.

'I was so shaken by this information, I took a carriage to Stirling and visited the family burial plot. Alongside Aunt's headstone was May Moray's: "Devoted Servant and Friend".

'Oh, how I wished you had been with me, dearest,' she said to Vince. 'I knew that we were in the hands of an imposter, although I had no notion why, but I had to let Rose know what had happened. So I took a train to Glasgow —'

Again she paused and Vince gave his stepfather a look that said how proud he was of his enterprising young wife.

'I went at once to Rose's lodging. Her landlady seemed surprised to see me when I said who I was. A couple of days earlier, a young woman, a maid, answering to the description of May, had come for her with a note. Rose left with her immediately, saying she was going to Dunblane.

'She had never arrived at Dunblane. That was three days ago and neither of them has been seen since. I panicked and rushed home, hoping to find them both here. And that someone would explain it all to me.'

Tearfully she looked up at Faro, as if he might have the magical solution. 'If she isn't May Moray, then who is she? And why has she been living in this house pretending to be her?' she whispered.

As the terrible pattern began to emerge, Faro could have supplied answers to several of their questions, answers that did little to comfort him and would have seriously increased Olivia's terrors. His greatest anxiety, however, concerned the safety of his daughter.

'If anything has happened to dearest Rose, then it's all my fault,' Olivia sobbed. 'All my fault for not telling you after Duddingston when everyone presumed I was out of sorts,' she paused and touched her stomach, 'because of the baby —'

And, flinging herself into her husband's arms, she looked at Faro and said hopefully, 'Have you any idea where they are?'

Vince stared at him over her head. 'We must find them, Stepfather. And quickly.'

If there had been room in his heart for any emotion but horror, Faro would have regarded the scene before him and the information he had been given with something akin to triumph.

He had been given a thread leading through the labyrinth. The first clue lay in the Stirling connections, a nest of Fenian activities according to McQuinn. And through some passing association with the real May — and he was not dismissing entirely that they had not been responsible for her death in some way. There were drugs that could simulate deadly fevers. Had she communicated Aunt Gilchrist's connections with Inspector Faro and someone had seen a golden opportunity of planting one of their members in his household, especially a detective responsible for saving the Queen from numerous Fenian attempts on her life?

The fact that the real May was dumb was an advantage. It saved the false May from concealing an Irish accent.

Watching Olivia being consoled by Vince, Faro's mind raced ahead. He guessed that Constable Thomas's sharp wits had enabled him to divine the truth of May's real identity. And that was the urgent message. He had indeed 'cracked the chief's case for him' but at the cost of his own life. At the 'maid's' instigation. Faro thought grimly.

And suddenly he sat upright.

The birthday present.

The package that Thomas had left to be delivered to May's bedside when she awoke. 'Poems he'd written, that sort of thing,' according to Mrs Brook.

He ran downstairs to the kitchen but the housekeeper was absent. He stood by the table recalling in meticulous detail what she had told him. How, when May had appeared, Thomas had tipped Mrs Brook a wink and said sternly that this was for Inspector Faro. Urgent.

Faro imagined the scene. May at the door, overhearing, had taken flight, believing that Thomas had somehow got hold of the Queen's journal. Perhaps besotted by her, he had been indiscreet about his investigations in the McNair murders.

'Put it on his desk,' Thomas had said.

Which was why May had seized the excuse of 'tidying' to ransack his study. Searching in vain, she had been convinced that Faro still had it in his possession.

And there was only one way to bargain with him.

Rose.

Rose as hostage.

Sick with apprehension, he steadied himself against the kitchen table, seeing the package in Mrs Brook's hand as she thrust it back into her sideboard drawer.

It was still there. Carrying it up to his study, he opened the envelope so expertly that it could be resealed again without anyone knowing the contents had been examined.

As he expected, it contained some papers and a small leather notebook.

He began to read.

Chapter Twenty-Three

Faro's reading was interrupted by the shrill ringing of the front doorbell. Within minutes he heard Vince telling the caller to wait, that he would get his bag and his instruments.

Two minutes later, the bell again jangled through the house.

Faro sprang to his feet. Could it be Rose, returned unharmed at last?

He opened the door to hear a man, rough voiced, speaking to Mrs Brook in urgent tones.

Another of Vince's emergencies, Faro thought, picking up the book again while downstairs Mrs Brook desperately confronted the gypsy beggarman who first wanted to tell her fortune and then wanted her to buy clothes pegs from him.

'Be off,' she said, bristling with rage as he put a foot in the door and, leaning forward confidentially, whispered, 'A cup of tea in your cosy kitchen then, ma'am, if you please.'

'How dare you suggest —' Mrs Brook was not long lost for words. 'The owner of this house is a detective inspector —'

But before she could protest further he murmured, 'Thank you kindly,' and, pushing her aside bolted up the stairs.

She puffed after him in hot pursuit, but before she could do more than scream a warning he had thrown open the door of Inspector Faro's study.

Warned by the commotion, Faro had time only to thrust the little book into the desk drawer where he could most conveniently lay hands on his revolver, ready to confront one of the Fenian terrorists.

The man who stood before him had one of the most villainous countenances Faro had ever beheld.

A black patch over one eye, hair an entangled mass that had seen neither comb nor water for many a long day, while all resemblance to recognizable garments had long since vanished into the shredded rags that covered him. The gold earring declared him a gypsy.

The man had seen Faro's movement towards the half-open drawer. Raising a finger he pointed. 'I shouldn't do that, sir, not if I was you.'

And, leering at him across the table, he nodded in Mrs Brook's direction. 'Send her packing,' he said roughly, putting a finger to his lips.

'Inspector, sir!' she protested.

Again the man shook his head, grinned, and that grin was familiar.

'It is all right, Mrs Brook. This er — fellow is known to me.' And as Mrs Brook hesitated, he led her gently to the door. 'Don't you worry. It's police business.'

Mrs Brook departed in a deep huff, muttering for all the house to hear, 'Police business indeed.' And that she didn't know what this house was coming to, really she didn't.

She would have been taken aback by the scene she had just left to see Inspector Faro dancing delightedly around the appalling beggarman.

'McQuinn!'

Like the answer to his prayers, McQuinn had arrived.

'I got your messages — both of them. Came as quickly as I could, sir.'

Handing him a dram, Faro related the events leading to Olivia's disclosures and the spy who had been infiltrated into his house.

But it was Rose's abduction that most concerned them both.

'We haven't much time,' said McQuinn, 'I know there's something big on. A ship leaves on the midnight tide for Rosslare and their ringleader will be on it — and if their plan goes well, the Queen's journal will be in her pocket.'

'I don't give a damn for any journal. All I want is my Rose safe home, do you hear.'

McQuinn looked grave. 'They're holding her as hostage. I'm glad I got here first.' He looked at the clock. 'Someone'll be arriving shortly. They don't have time to waste. Once they have what they came for, they'll be off for Ireland.'

'How can we stop them?'

'The answer is that we can't — it's the journal or Rose. We don't really have a choice, do we?' So saying, he held out his hand.

Faro watched him as he turned the pages, smiling as if the contents amused him.

Then he pushed it back across the table. 'Let

them have this, Inspector. It's our only hope. Do what they want, I'll be keeping watch.'

McQuinn nodded towards the window. 'I seem to remember there's a way out across the wash-house roof into the back lane.'

'Yes, but be careful.'

'Sure now, Inspector, have you ever known me not to be?'

McQuinn's soft laughter, his mockery, infuriated Faro. How could he take it all lightly with so much at stake?

'McQuinn!' he said sharply.

'Yes, sir?'

'If — if it all goes wrong. Save Rose. That's an order, do you hear?'

'Inspector, sir, you hardly need to tell me that. She's the girl I intend making my wife.' He pointed to the book. 'Give it to them,' he repeated sternly. 'And God save Ireland.'

McQuinn had not been gone more than a minute when the front doorbell rang yet again. Faro thrust the book and the loose papers into his pocket as Mrs Brook came upstairs.

She opened the door and seemed surprised to see him alone.

'There's a lady to see you, sir. I put her in the dining room, sir, thinking you already had a — a — visitor,' she added reproachfully with a quick look round as if to see whether such a creature's presence might have sullied her much polished furniture.

Faro followed her downstairs.

He opened the door. The shadowy figure by the window moved.

It was Imogen Crowe.

For a moment his heart beat wildly, the images in his mind those of a fantasy come true. Imogen had changed her mind. His blood leaped at the thought. She wanted him, this meeting had nothing to do with Fenians or with his daughter Rose, their hostage.

But even as she turned to face him, he knew that relief from the agony of a doomed love was not yet to be his.

Her face was expressionless, a mirror from which all emotion had been wiped clean.

'What have you done with my daughter?' he gasped.

'If you want to see Rose again, you had better come with me and bring the Queen's journal with you.'

'Where is my daughter?'

'At Leith. I'm to take you there.'

And at his stricken face, she showed her first compassion. 'Rose is perfectly all right. Not a hair of her head has been harmed, so far. She is a very brave girl, your daughter. But that's to be expected.'

'Why Leith?' he asked, knowing the answer perfectly well.

'It's too dangerous to remain in Scotland. Besides, they have other plans and some of the group have been already rounded up. They might still need Rose as a safe conduct.'

And Rose would never reach Ireland, Faro thought in grim despair. There would be a convenient accident. A woman lost overboard.

'And you are to be held responsible for their villainous plans — for my daughter's murder.'

In reply she looked at him. 'Believe what you will. I'm here to try to save her if I can. It all depends on you, Inspector. All they want is the Queen's journal.'

'How are you so sure I have it?'

Imogen smiled. 'Maeve — May you called her — heard that constable who was courting her tell Mrs Brook to put it on your desk. You hid it pretty well.' Pausing, she glanced around the room.

'Maeve searched everywhere, your desk and cupboards, but she couldn't find it. I suppose you have a secret safe somewhere. I hope for Rose's sake that you have it with you this night —'

And as Faro touched his pocket in an involuntary gesture, she smiled. 'Ah, I see I was right. Now shall we go?'

As he followed her out towards the waiting carriage, reason told him to hate her, to destroy her. But as they sat together in the darkness her perfume, her beloved presence, reached out to him and mocked him again with the madness of desire never now to be fulfilled.

Chapter Twenty-Four

'You are to come unarmed. You are to tell no one of your destination. If you disobey and alert your colleagues then our people will kill Rose.'

Faro did not doubt for a moment that Imogen's deadly warning was in earnest as he struggled to make excuses for her. She had every reason to hate the English and he recognized over and over again the declaration of her unswerving loyalty to the Fenians. Just two words proudly said: 'Our people.'

Emotions were too deep to allow conversation that would not fast deteriorate — on Faro's side — to reproach and recrimination and, as the carriage reached the quayside at Leith, he saw that the *Erin Star*, a ship with whose movements he was well acquainted was preparing to leave for Rosslare on the evening tide. He guessed this was to be their escape route back to Ireland. They had taken few chances of their careful plan failing by sending Imogen for him as late as possible.

Then he noticed ahead of the *Erin Star* the yacht the *Royal Solent* bound for the Isle of Wight. And more significantly that the Queen was resident at Osborne House.

At Faro's side Imogen regarded the yacht anxiously from the carriage window. Her expression and the fact that there were few signs of departure evident on deck aroused Faro's suspicions that the Fenians had already overpowered the crew and that Osborne House with its unprotected shoreline would be the scene of the next assassination attempt.

He sat back. Time was running out. He had now less than half an hour, his wits and the precious package he carried, to save his daughter.

As they left the carriage, two men moved out of the shadows and took a firm grip on his arms. Unable to twist round and see their faces, for a moment he thought he was back in the hands of his attackers in the Mound, the killers of the McNairs who had also skilfully evaded him in Stirling Railway Station.

They had also tried to murder Imogen and automatically his fists bunched and he struggled violently to escape from their hold.

Then Imogen spoke to them in Gaelic, obviously telling them to release him.

'You are to be blindfolded,' she said. 'Don't be alarmed.'

'It is a safety measure only,' said one of the men and turning Faro saw that the pair were little more than youths, slightly built, with the look of brothers. He could have felled the two of them with little trouble.

'Our work here is not finished,' said the taller of the two. 'And we may wish to return.'

Their heavily accented voices were cultured and as they led him across what was undoubtedly a cobbled yard, he should have felt heartened until he realized that educated fanatics can be equally deadly as ignorant villains.

A door creaked and opened, footsteps, another door and then a sound like a panel being slid along and he was guided into a room where the voices ceased as he entered.

'Rose? Where are you?'

'Pa, oh Pa.' The dearest words in the world were followed by, 'What have they done to you?'

'We haven't harmed him,' said Imogen.

But he couldn't reach Rose, his captors held his arms. There were several people in the room speaking Gaelic. Again he recognized Imogen's voice. He remembered McQuinn saying he knew only that their leader was a woman, clever, intelligent.

That could only be Imogen Crowe. Fool that he was to love — to have loved — such a one.

Suddenly there was a buzz of activity around him, the scraping of heavy boxes across the floor. He was in some sort of a warehouse. He sniffed the air, the acrid smell he associated with ammunition. So this was the secret place where bombs were being made.

Bombs, he did not doubt, that were destined for the Isle of Wight and Osborne House. Guns too, for he heard the rattle of steel, the sound of nails being driven home.

A sudden stillness, then another woman's voice, speaking rapidly in Gaelic, then in English giving instructions: 'Get going. It will take you all your time to load these. They are ready to weigh anchor.'

He sniffed the air again, the smell of burning paper.

Footsteps approached, light ones this time, and the blindfold was pulled from his eyes. He blinked, searching for Rose, in the dim illumination from a couple of hanging lanterns.

She sat on an upturned box across the room, the woman bending over her removing the blindfold. Rose sat up, saw him, and with a delighted cry she pushed her captor roughly aside and a moment later she was close in his embrace.

But brave Rose gave way at last. She sobbed quietly, trembling against him.

Over her shoulder, Faro saw that the room had emptied of the gunmen taking their cargo to the ship. The smell of burning, no doubt of incriminating documents, came from the other side of the room where the two brothers were busily thrusting papers into a stove.

Imogen talked quietly to the woman who turned to face him. The woman who had called herself May Moray.

Faro was amazed as she approached. Amazed at the transformation from the shy, frightened maid to the confident terrorist. She seemed to have grown in stature as well as authority. She would never have beauty, but she had power. Her lack of distinctive features, which would not be remembered as would Imogen Crowe's, was an adequate disguise, a blessing for any criminal.

The door opened. A man peered round at them. 'We have to leave.' It was said in Gaelic but the urgency was unmistakable in any language.

Maeve held out her hand to Faro. 'You have the journal.'

Faro nodded and touched his pocket. She smiled. 'You are wise, Inspector Faro. Now give it to me, then you and your daughter are free to go. She —' Her head swivelled in Imogen's direction. 'She has guaranteed your safe conduct.'

Faro stared at Imogen's expressionless face.

She shrugged. 'A debt to be paid, that's all, Inspector Faro. Now I owe you nothing.'

'The journal,' said Maeve. 'We've wasted enough time.'

He took it out of his pocket. As she stretched out her hand, he seized her in a stranglehold. Powerless, she screamed.

'I can break her neck in one,' Faro said grimly. 'So let Rose go.'

The two brothers took a step forward, wavered. For a moment they were frozen in a tableau, a play from which the cues had been lost, the actors in confusion.

As for Faro, he had to rely on the slender hope that Imogen meant no harm to Rose and himself. Pushing Maeve before him as a shield while she cursed and struggled against him, powerless in his iron grip, he edged towards the brightly burning stove.

At that moment the panel slid open, the two men who were his old enemies exploded into the room. He saw the rifles raised pointing at him. He heard Maeve scream once, then she went limp in his arms.

She slid to the ground as he released her, frantically reaching out for Rose, her safety his chief concern. The two men rushed forward, hands outstretched, and Faro realized that he still held in one hand the journal that Maeve had died for.

As they approached he threw it, a neatly calculated throw, which he prayed would reach its target. They yelled abuse at him as it disappeared into the open stove. No longer interested in him, they rushed towards the flames, hoping to be in time to save it before it was consumed and changed into ashes.

Faro managed to trip the first one *en route*. Seizing his rifle he helped him to the floor by felling him with one blow to the back of the neck. As the second man rushed towards him protesting, he brought the rifle down with a resounding crack against the side of his head.

Savouring for a moment the sense of satisfaction as his two attackers lay senseless before him, he turned and saw Imogen, her arms outstretched, protecting Rose, whom she had thrust behind her.

There was no movement from Maeve, who lay motionless where she had fallen, a stream of blood oozing from her breast.

The sound of footsteps and Faro again raised the rifle.

The beggarman —

McQuinn rushed in. Ignoring Faro, he ran to Rose's side. He touched her hair briefly as if to reassure himself that she was unharmed.

Rose screamed, failing to recognize him, and Imogen thumped him with her fists. 'Leave her alone — leave her.'

McQuinn laughed as Rose cowered away from him, suspecting another terrorist. Holding Imogen at bay with one hand, he held out the other to Rose. 'Darlin' — it's me — your Danny.'

'Danny — you idiot!' Half laughing, half crying, she disentangled herself from Imogen and briefly kissed him.

Then with a shake of his head he ran over to where Maeve lay.

'She's dead. They killed her,' said Faro, standing with his rifle poised over the two men who groaned on the floor. 'And they'd have had me too.'

'It was her they wanted. Not you,' said McQuinn.

But Faro wasn't listening. Turning, he saw that Rose had disappeared with Imogen and the two brothers.

He rushed towards the open panel. 'Come along, McQuinn. You know the way. I was blindfolded. Come on —'

McQuinn led the way through the doors out of the old warehouse until they stood on the now empty quayside where the lights of the *Erin Star* and the *Royal Solent* moved swiftly towards the harbour bar.

Faro watched them helplessly.

The Fenians had escaped. But they had taken Rose with them.

'They won't get far,' said McQuinn.

'Dear God, man, why didn't you stop them!' he shouted angrily, as a figure emerged from the shadows.

It was Imogen.

'I put Rose into the police carriage. Over there. She's waiting for you.'

'What about the yacht?' Faro yelled and McQuinn shouted something that was lost as he ran to the carriage.

Faro watched as he took Rose in his arms. He heard her laughter. 'Danny McQuinn, you smell. When did you last have a bath?'

Rose was safe.

He turned to Imogen, standing silently at his side, and nodded towards the fast disappearing ships.

'They went without you.'

'You sound surprised, Inspector.' She shrugged. 'I've served my purpose. I got you here, got the journal for them. And I wouldn't be much use to them on the Isle of Wight.'

'So I was right. That's where they're heading.'

'It's been planned for a long time. They are nothing if not meticulous, despite what the English pretend about the stupid Irish,' she said bitterly.

'What are you going to do now? Those two men back there —' he added, indicating the black outline of the warehouse. 'If they survive, they'll kill you this time.'

She nodded. 'I know. I know.'

'I thought you were the leader,' he said apologetically.

'Me?' she laughed. 'Heavens, no. They enlisted me — reluctantly I have to add — as a go-between. I had little choice with Seamus's wife and bairn back in Ireland, waiting to be murdered if I didn't obey their instructions. They don't make idle threats; you should know that by now.'

'Tell me something, why did you come back to the hotel in Stirling that day and ask for me?'

She shrugged. 'An impulse. I was passing by, and I suddenly needed to say I was sorry — sorry that things had to end that way between us.' She looked up at him sadly. 'But you had gone, I was too late. Fate was never on our side. Perhaps it was just as well.'

There were other questions in the air, but survival left no time for explanations.

'You'll be taken,' Faro said urgently. 'You'll go to prison and I won't be able to help you this time. You must get away.'

'You should care,' she said bitterly.

He looked at her, put his hand on her arm. 'I do care, Imogen.' And the words unspoken: Please God, you will never know how much.

The darkness across the water was pierced by a siren whistle. McQuinn rushed past them.

'That's the *Solent*. The Harbour Police have

218

stopped her. Thank God my message got through in time.'

He looked at Imogen. 'And thank you, lady, for looking after my Rose.' And to Faro he shouted over his shoulder as he ran along the quayside, 'I leave it to you, sir, to arrest her.'

Faro's mind was working rapidly. The distant lights and the commotion along the quayside told him that the yacht had been ahead of the passenger ship. Imogen had one chance.

'How good are you with a rowing boat?'

'Glory be, Inspector, you don't expect me to row all the way back to Ireland?'

'Don't argue. Come along, we haven't a minute to lose.' And, dragging her by the arm, he ran down the steps and thrust her into a small fishing boat. Turning it adrift they both took to the oars. He cut short Imogen's protests. 'The captain will stop for me. Being a policeman has its uses and we've had dealings before.'

There was no time for explanations or promises. All their energies were needed to row across to where the *Erin Star* would head out of harbour and into the North Sea, down around the English coast and to Rosslare where Imogen would be safe. Safe but out of his life for ever.

As Faro hailed the ship, they rocked unsteadily in the swell, the bows poised dangerously above them. The captain stared down from the bridge, then the searchlight picked out the rowing boat and Inspector Faro.

'Another passenger for you, captain. Sling

down the ladder, if you please.'

Reaching out his hand to seize it and to help Imogen as she transferred from the rowing boat, he asked, 'Have you money for your fare?'

She laughed. 'What a practical man you are, Inspector. We're snatched from the jaws of death and you ask whether I can pay for my passage.'

Smiling in return, he held her briefly for the last time.

'I wonder if I'll ever see you again,' she said softly.

'Promises, promises. Remember the last time — Berwick Station, it was.'

'You can always come to Ireland.'

'Who knows? Maybe I will,' said Faro as, leaning forward, she kissed him full on the mouth and began to climb the swaying ladder.

Chapter Twenty-Five

McQuinn was waiting for him at the quayside as he moored the rowing boat and climbed the steps alone.

'I see you caught the *Erin Star*. Well done, sir. I sent Rose home to Sheridan Place. She'll be waiting for you there.'

As the two men fell into step and headed in the direction of the lights of Edinburgh, Faro, who was bone weary, would have given much for the sight of a carriage.

'What happened here?'

'The Harbour Police intercepted the *Royal Solent*, put the bad lads away and released a very frightened crew who have now continued their journey to the Isle of Wight.' He stopped and laughed. 'With those members of the Royal entourage who had imagined there were fewer hazards by sea than land and were very badly scared —'

'Why wasn't I warned about all this?' Faro interrupted angrily.

'Because of Rose, sir. Central Office was afraid that with your daughter's safety involved you might do something — well, impulsive. Such as trying a single-handed rescue. It has been known, sir.'

Faro swore at him as with a grin he continued,

'I tried to reach you at Sheridan Place, to reassure you. But I was too late. Mrs Brook said you had left with Miss Crowe.'

He sighed. 'I was glad I was wrong about Miss Crowe. I didn't trust her and neither did the Fenians, but they had an effective weapon in using her family in Ireland as blackmail. Then Rose told me how she had protected her and even worked out a plan to help her escape at the risk of her own life.' McQuinn shrugged. 'Not that it would have made any difference, she would still have gone to prison. If things had worked out differently.' He laughed softly. 'She has a lot to thank you for this night, sir.'

'What about you, McQuinn. What now?'

'My job is finished.' And ruefully rubbing his chin, he added, 'Shave off the beard, have a much needed bath.' He sighed. 'And then America. As I intended. I need a change of air.'

'What about Rose? Are you considering her in these plans?'

A street lamp illuminated McQuinn's face briefly. He smiled. 'She has to decide. It's up to her. I want to marry her but it has to be on my terms. As one plain policeman to another, if you'll forgive me for once not acknowledging your illustrious rank and experience, you know that's the truth.'

'You mean that the job comes first.'

'You take my meaning exactly, sir.'

They walked slowly, silently, their footsteps echoing on the now empty pavements.

'Have you ever considered that Rose might find someone else while you are away?'

McQuinn frowned. 'Someone like Lachlan Brown, you mean.'

Conscious of Faro's startled glance, McQuinn laughed. 'I know all about Lachlan Brown, her letters were full of him. A dose of hero worship, I'd say.'

Another silence followed this revelation. 'Our two murderers back there in the warehouse, I presume they are safely under lock and key for me to interview in the morning. I'll have enough in my report to hang them both,' said Faro grimly.

McQuinn shrugged. 'They'll have sore heads and that's about all, sir.' And, at Faro's angry explosion, 'They're on our side.'

'Indeed. They tried to kill Lachlan Brown, so whose side is he on?'

'It was McNair they were after. They nabbed him leaving the Assembly Rooms, didn't know how much he'd told Lachlan and that a warning might be timely. Just obeying orders, sir.'

'Whose orders?' Faro demanded.

'Those of a higher authority, sir. And you know the identity of that higher authority better than most. God knows she has more reason to be grateful to you than most of us.'

Faro stopped walking. He felt suddenly sick at the significance of McQuinn's remarks, as he added:

'They are very high-ranking officers in her security force, sir.'

McQuinn paused to let his words sink in and then said gently, 'Everyone who knew the contents of the journal was a threat. Even a respectable and greatly prized Chief Inspector is expendable when the throne is in danger.'

'They made that plain enough when they took a pot shot at me in Stirling,' said Faro bitterly. 'And they had doubtless taken into account that I was suspect having taken Imogen Crowe, a known terrorist, on an outing to Inchmahome.'

'You were under constant surveillance, sir. Regardless of all you've done in the past risking your life for the monarchy, that's all the thanks you — or any of us — can expect.' And McQuinn muttered something under his breath. It sounded suspiciously seditious, like: God save Ireland.

Faro knew it was true. He had been involved in a very similar situation when he tried to prove that his policeman father had been murdered — because he knew too much to keep Royal posteriors at ease on the throne of England.

He found, however, that he was not as expendable as McQuinn believed.

Superintendent McIntosh was to retire that summer and hints reached Chief Inspector Faro that he was to be offered his job. Which he had no intention of accepting, guessing that it was a ruse to get him safely behind a desk and away from embarrassing situations such as the McNair murders.

No doubt the whisper had been: Let him work

at such matters in theory only, where we can keep an eye on him.

Meanwhile he returned to the routine crimes that made up the majority of his cases and his domestic life settled down into its usual ordered existence with Mrs Brook once again a contented woman in the kitchen where she ruled alone and supreme.

The recent drama involving a Sheridan Place servant had confirmed her belief that maids were trouble and, wise after the event, she wasn't surprised to find that May Moray had been an impostor and possibly a murderess too.

'There was something about her, Inspector. I never liked her.'

Meanwhile Vince and Olivia resumed their joyful expectations planning for the new baby while Rose returned to Glasgow in a happy glow about McQuinn, the hero who had rescued her for the second time in her life. She declined, however, to comment on whether she would be marrying him when he returned from America.

As for Faro, he was surprised to realize that he was ready to welcome Sergeant Danny McQuinn as a desirable and suitable son-in-law. All his former doubts had vanished, but he remained in constant anxiety that Rose, in Danny's long absence, might yet choose Lachlan Brown.

A week after the newspapers had exhausted 'Fenian Terrorists Captured' and 'Leith Warehouse Destroyed by Fire', Faro was at work on

225

less sensational matters when he had two surprising visits.

He found Sir Hamish Royston Blunt awaiting an interview with him at the Central Office.

Aware that he was visiting Edinburgh on official business connected with his Parliamentary activities, Faro asked what the Police could do for him.

Sir Hamish shook his head and smiled.

'This is a purely personal visit. And a sad one, I'm afraid,' he added, handing Faro a small velvet box. Watching him open it Sir Hamish said, 'It is, I believe, a Viking ring and Inga asked me when I was next in Edinburgh to give it to you for its safe return to Orkney.'

'Inga — St Ola?' said Faro. 'I had no idea you two were acquainted.'

Sir Hamish regarded him sadly across the table. 'Inga was my wife.'

Faro's astonishment at this news faded rapidly at Sir Hamish's grief-stricken expression.

'Is she — is she — ?'

Sir Hamish nodded. 'She died a week ago. Lachlan was with her at the end.' He paused and then said, 'Lachlan is our son.'

At Faro's startled glance, he said, 'We weren't actually married, although it was my dearest wish. As you may know, I have been a respected Minister for some years. You may also be aware that I had a wife and a grown-up family.

'I was living in Glasgow, a Junior Minister with a promising career when Inga came to work for us from Orkney. We fell in love. I wanted to

226

marry her when I knew she was to have my child. Mine had been an arranged marriage, without great passion but with a great deal of affection and respect on both sides. Neither my wife nor myself had ever pretended it was a grand passion, but Inga knew that divorce would ruin my career.

'And she could not bear to inflict such misery on my wife who had been so good to her — and my children whom she loved. She knew the scandal would blight all their lives, destroy the respect they had for a father whom they believed to be good and true.'

He paused. 'One day she disappeared. I was frantic but I had no idea where to look for her. I set discreet agencies to work to find her. And at last I walked into a boarding house where I found her with my baby son. She had decided to return to Orkney and, as I am not without influence, I persuaded her to let a childless couple in John Brown's family bring him up. That way I could keep an eye on him when I was at Balmoral.

'My wife never knew of Lachlan's existence. She died five years ago at the time Lachlan began his career. I met Inga in his dressing room in London last year and we discovered we still loved each other. Such a discovery, and then she told me she had only a little time left. She was incurably ill. Nevertheless I insisted that we should be married. You know the rest.'

As he talked Faro realized the reason Sir Hamish had seemed so familiar when they met in the Stirling courthouse. All these years since he first met Lachlan he had been tormenting himself that Inga's son was also his, but he could not mistake Lachlan's physical resemblance to his real father, even his gestures, head and hand movements were the same.

Yet Inga had never told him the truth. She had been his first love. He had left her and she had never forgotten or forgiven him. Now he understood. She had her revenge, he thought, opening the velvet box.

He had almost forgotten the ring he had given her. They found it on the beach in Kirkwall where they had first made love. It had seemed like a good omen. Inga had laughed and said she would keep it always and it was as if the old Viking gods blessed them.

There was a note folded beside the ring: 'Dear Jeremy, By the time this reaches you, you will have heard the whole story from Hamish. And an answer to an old riddle. Inga.'

Now he need worry no longer if Rose chose Lachlan. Or hoped that he was putting the right interpretation on Inga's note. Inga had always been an enigma. Love and Lachlan had not changed her.

Faro had hardly recovered from the shock of Sir Hamish's revelations when a second visitor arrived at the Central Office.

'There's a lady waiting for you. In your office, sir,' said the desk constable.

For a moment his heart leaped. He raced down

the corridor. This could only mean one thing. The miracle he had prayed for had happened — Imogen had returned.

Chapter Twenty-Six

Faro threw open the door to his office and discovered the last person he ever wished to see again.

Mrs Carling, with the reluctant surly-faced Andy cowering at her side. She thrust him forward.

'Go on. Tell the Inspector.' She quelled his rebellious look by adding shrilly, 'There's been killings involved, murder most like. I don't want you, or my house, mixed up in it. I worked hard for you all these years, trying to give you a respectable life after your father left us and went to prison. He died there.'

She paused and looked at Faro helplessly. 'It was fraud he was in for, Inspector, and I don't want my lad to go the same way, really I don't. It would break my heart. He's not much —' she said with an angry look in his direction, 'but he's all I've got and he has good in him, of that I'm sure. I took my maiden name and I've slaved all my life trying to keep him out of trouble. And I'm not throwing it all away now.'

So saying, she seized Andy and shook him none too gently. 'Do you hear your mother when she's speaking to you?' She emphasized her words by cuffing him sharply across the ears. 'Tell the Inspector, Andy Carling, or you're no son of mine and you'll leave my house and never come back to it. Do you understand what I'm saying?'

Andy nodded feebly.

'You'd better. Because I mean every word of it.'

'All right, Ma. All right.'

Mrs Carling turned to Faro. 'Andy has something to show you, Inspector. I discovered it hidden in his room when I was cleaning. Under the mattress it was, deceitful young devil,' she screamed at him, waving a threatening fist inches from his nose.

And from her reticule she took out a large envelope and pushed it across the desk.

Faro picked it up. The address read: Miss McNair, Holly Cottage, Duddingston.

'He was paid handsomely by poor Mr Glen to deliver it to her, but he never did. He kept the money instead. Then when poor Mr Glen died and he discovered the cottage was burnt, and the police were interested, he got the idea that there was trouble and that he might be involved. Then when that constable was stabbed he lost his nerve. When I saw the seals an' all, I thought it might be valuable.'

'Do you know what this packet contains?' Faro asked Andy.

Andy looked uncomfortable and exchanged a glance with his mother who wasn't going to help him. 'Just a wee book wi' writing, poetry and suchlike,' he added contemptuously. Obviously he had been bitterly disappointed in the contents.

'I've told him a thousand times,' Mrs Carling interrupted, 'I'll kill him if he gets into trouble with the Police and brings disgrace on me after all I've suffered in the past. I've hardly slept at nights since I knew Andy had this.'

They were both obviously very scared and with good reason, thought Faro, guessing that the envelope contained the missing Royal journal, and the love letters exchanged between the Queen and John Brown, stolen by Bessie McNair when she was repairing the Royal riding dress in Balmoral.

'Is it valuable, mister?' Andy's eyes gleamed.

'It might well be that there is a reward for it,' said Faro and he unlocked a drawer and took out ten sovereigns, which he handed across the desk.

Mrs Carling was voluble in her thanks and practically took it on herself to swear to keep Andy a law-abiding citizen in future.

Seeing them out, Faro inspected the envelope, which had been carefully opened and resealed. Doubtless it would never have been returned had it contained, as the pair had hoped, money which would have been quickly pocketed.

It was unlikely that Mrs Carling realized the true significance of 'poetry and suchlike' or the author's true identity. As for Andy, Faro suspected that his reading capabilities were severely limited.

It was a bright day heading towards a magnificent sunset over the city skyline and he decided to walk home through Holyrood Park. On the tiny loch below St Anthony's Chapel, swans sailed, remote as magical creatures from a fairy tale. An Irish legend, he remembered had turned seven princes, the sons of Usna, into swans.

Tonight he could believe it, but it didn't bring Imogen back to him.

Sitting on a rock near the rippling surface of the waters, he opened the envelope and took out the journal. Reading anyone's private and intimate thoughts filled him with distaste and anger too, at the lives this little book had cost, but curiosity overcame his scruples.

It did not take the scanning of many pages to realize that if the information it held was made public, this could bring down the throne.

The words leaped out at him: John Brown addressed as 'husband of my heart' and 'secret vows taken together'. He had read enough. If these words were true and not the fantasies of a lovesick woman, then they signified the existence of a secret marriage, long suspected.

He closed the book and stood at the water's edge. Authority now believed the journal had been safely destroyed by him, burnt to ashes in the stove during the warehouse siege at Leith.

Let them continue to believe it.

Only one other person guessed the truth.

Imogen Crowe.

And he remembered how, safely aboard the *Erin Star*, she leaned over the rail and, looking down at him, she had laughed.

'You're a sly one, Inspector, so you are. Seamus described the Queen's journal as bright blue leather with the Royal insignia. The one in your hand was red. So what was that little book you threw into the stove back there?'

And the ship's siren drowned out his reply. That he had burned Constable Thomas's love poems to his traitorous sweetheart.

Now he lifted his arm and threw the journal as far as it would go, watching it skim across the water, its pages fluttering open briefly to be pulled down into the depths of the loch.

The swans circled curiously at this disturbance then they too lost interest. Faro lingered for a moment but there was no Arthurian magic here, no arm arose from the waters clutching the fatal journal in its hand.

And, turning, he walked briskly homewards.

We hope you have enjoyed this Large Print book. Other G.K. Hall & Co. or Chivers Press Large Print books are available at your library or directly from the publishers.

For more information about current and up-coming titles, please call or write, without obligation, to:

G.K. Hall & Co.
P.O. Box 159
Thorndike, Maine 04986 USA
Tel. (800) 223-2336

OR

Chivers Press Limited
Windsor Bridge Road
Bath BA2 3AX
England
Tel. (0225) 335336

All our Large Print titles are designed for easy reading, and all our books are made to last.